MAMA'S
BANK ACCOUNT

KATHRYN FORBES

SCHOLASTIC BOOK SERVICES
New York Toronto London Auckland Sydney Tokyo

ISBN: 0-590-09927-2

Copyright 1943 by Kathryn Forbes. Copyright © 1971 by Richard E. McLean and Robert M. McLean. This edition is published by Scholastic Book Services, a division of Scholastic Magazines, Inc., by arrangement with Harcourt Brace Jovanovich, Inc.

13 12 11 10 9 8 7 6 5 4 3   2 3 4 5 6/8

Printed in U.S.A.

01

FOR MAMA
FOR BOB
AND FOR THE MC LEAN BOYS

CONTENTS

1 ?? *Mama*
and Her Bank Account

For as long as I could remember, the small cottage on Castro Street had been home. The familiar background was there: Mama, Papa, my only brother, Nels. There was my sister Christine, closest to me in age, yet ever secret and withdrawn — and the littlest sister, Dagmar.

There, too, came the Aunts, Mama's four sisters. Aunt Jenny, who was the oldest and the bossiest; Aunt Sigrid; Aunt Marta; and our maiden Aunt, Trina.

The Aunts' old bachelor uncle, my Greatuncle Chris — the "black Norwegian" — came with his great impatience, his shouting and stamping. And brought mystery and excitement to our humdrum days.

But the first awareness was of Mama.

I remember that every Saturday night Mama would sit down by the scrubbed kitchen table and with much wrinkling of usually placid brows count out the money Papa had brought home in the little envelope.

There would be various stacks.

"For the landlord," Mama would say, piling up the big silver pieces.

"For the grocer." Another group of coins.

"For Katrin's shoes to be half-soled." And Mama would count out the little silver.

"Teacher says this week I'll need a notebook." That would be Christine or Nels or I.

Mama would solemnly detach a nickel or a dime and set it aside.

We would watch the diminishing pile with breathless interest.

At last, Papa would ask, "Is all?"

And when Mama nodded, we could relax a little and reach for schoolbooks and homework. For Mama would look up and then smile. "Is good," she'd murmur. "We do not have to go to the Bank."

It was a wonderful thing, that Bank Account of Mama's. We were all so proud of it. It gave us such warm, secure feeling. No one else we knew had money in a big bank downtown.

I remember when the Jensens down the street were put out because they couldn't pay their rent. We children watched the big strange men carry out the furniture, took furtive notice of poor Mrs. Jensen's shamed tears, and I

2

was choked with sudden fear. This, then, happened to people who did not have the stack of coins marked "Landlord." Might this, could this, violence happen to us?

I clutched Christine's hands. "*We* have a Bank Account," she reassured me calmly, and suddenly I could breathe again.

When Nels graduated from grammar school he wanted to go on to high. "Is good," Mama said, and Papa nodded approvingly.

"It will cost a little money," Nels said.

Eagerly we brought up chairs and gathered around the table. I took down the gaily painted box that Aunt Sigrid had sent us from Norway one Christmas and laid it carefully in front of Mama.

This was the "Little Bank." Not to be confused, you understand, with the Big Bank downtown. The Little Bank was used for sudden emergencies, such as the time Christine broke her arm and had to be taken to a doctor, or when Dagmar got croup and Papa had to go to the drugstore for medicine to put into the steam kettle.

Nels had it all written out neatly. So much for carfare, for clothes, for notebooks and supplies. Mama looked at the figures for a long time. Then she counted out the money in the Little Bank. There was not enough.

She pursed her lips. "We do not," she reminded us gently, "want to have to go to the Bank."

We all shook our heads.

"I will work in Dillon's grocery after school," Nels volunteered.

Mama gave him a bright smile and laboriously wrote down a sum and added and subtracted. Papa did it in his head. He was very quick on arithmetic. "Is not enough," he said. Then he took his pipe out of his mouth and looked at it for a long time. "I give up tobacco," he said suddenly.

Mama reached across the table and touched Papa's sleeve, but she didn't say anything. Just wrote down another figure.

"I will mind the Elvington children every Friday night," I said. "Christine can help me."

"Is good," Mama said.

We all felt very good. We had passed another milestone without having to go downtown and draw money out of Mama's Bank Account. The Little Bank was sufficient for the present.

So many things, I remember, came out of the Little Bank that year. Christine's costume for the school play, Dagmar's tonsil operation, my Girl Scout uniform. And always, in the background, was the comforting knowledge that should our efforts fail, we still had the Bank to depend upon.

Even when the strike came, Mama would

not let us worry unduly. We all worked together so that the momentous trip downtown could be postponed. It was almost like a game.

During that time Mama "helped out" at Kruper's bakery for a big sack of only slightly stale bread and coffee cake. And as Mama said, fresh bread was not too good for a person and if you put the coffee cake into the hot oven it was nearly as nice as when first baked.

Papa washed bottles at the Castro Creamery every night and they gave him three quarts of fresh milk and all the sour milk he could carry away. Mama made fine cheese.

The day the strike was over and Papa went back to work, I saw Mama stand a little straighter, as if to get a kink out of her back.

She looked around at us proudly. "Is *good*," she smiled. "See? We did not have to go down to the Bank."

That was twenty years ago.

Last year I sold my first story. When the check came I hurried over to Mama's and put the long green slip of paper in her lap. "For you," I said, "to put in your Bank Account."

And I noticed for the first time how old Mama and Papa looked. Papa seemed shorter, now, and Mama's wheaten braids were sheened with silver.

Mama fingered the check and looked at Papa.

"Is good," she said, and her eyes were proud.

"Tomorrow," I told her, "you must take it down to the Bank."

"You will go with me, Katrin?"

"That won't be necessary, Mama. See? I've endorsed the check to you. Just hand it to the teller, he'll deposit it to your account."

Mama looked at me. "Is no account," she said. "In all my life, I never been inside a Bank."

And when I didn't — couldn't — answer, Mama said earnestly: "Is not *good* for little ones to be afraid — to not feel secure."

2 ॐ *Mama*
and the Idle Roomer

Finances were low for many months after the strike.

Not that we were to worry, Mama told us, but would we mind having to move the davenport into the kitchen so that we could rent the front room?

We didn't mind, especially after Mama promised that with the money she got she would buy herself the warm coat she needed so badly.

Mr. Hyde called in answer to the neat "Room for Rent" sign in the window.

Mama and I showed him the room. Probably because it was Mama's first experience in renting, she forgot to ask for references or payment in advance.

"The quarters are eminently satisfactory." Mr. Hyde had such a refined way of speaking. "I'll have my bags sent up this evening. And my books."

Mr. Hyde fitted smoothly into our midst.

True, he didn't seem to have any regular hours of business. But he always spoke pleasantly to the children, and whenever he passed Mama in the hall he bowed gallantly.

Papa liked him too. Mr. Hyde had visited Norway once and could talk with Papa about the wonderful fishing there.

Only Aunt Jenny, who had a boardinghouse of her own, disapproved. "When," she asked, "is he going to pay his rent?"

"Is hard," Mama said, "to ask. Surely he will pay soon."

But Aunt Jenny only hmphed. She'd seen his kind before, she told us darkly. Mama needn't think she'd be able to buy any new coat with the rent she'd get from *that one*. Gentleman? Hmph!

Now that worried us children. But Mama smiled at our long faces. "Such talk," she scolded, and made coffee for Aunt Jenny to stop her grumbling.

When the rainy weather came, Mama worried that Mr. Hyde's room was cold in the evenings, so she had Papa invite him into the warm kitchen to sit with us. Christine, Nels, and I did our homework under the big lamp, and Papa and Mr. Hyde smoked their pipes by the stove. Mama worked quietly at the sink, setting the bread or making clabber cheese.

Mr. Hyde advised Nels on his high school

courses and sometimes helped him with his Latin. Nels became interested, his grades improved, and he stopped begging Papa to let him quit school and go to work.

After we finished our schoolwork and Mama had settled down in the rocking chair with her mending, Mr. Hyde would tell us of his travels and adventures. Oh, he knew so many things! It was like history and geography coming to life and marching around the room. Mr. Hyde had gone to Oxford and had sailed all around the world.

One night he began to read Dickens to us. Soon it became an accepted fact that after our homework was done, Mr. Hyde would bring down one of his books and read aloud. And strange new worlds were opened to us.

"They are like sagas," Mama said. "Wonderful."

After *David Copperfield* and *The Old Curiosity Shop*, Mr. Hyde gave us Shakespeare. He had a fine deep voice and sounded as we imagined a great actor would sound.

Even when the warm weather came we children didn't beg to go out in the evenings to play one-foot-off-the-gutter. I think Mama was glad; she never liked us running the streets.

Best of all, Nels went less and less to the street corner to hang around with the neighborhood boys. The night they got into trouble for breaking into Mr. Dillon's store Nels was home with us. He'd wanted to hear the last chapter of *Dombey and Son*.

Mr. Hyde had taken us deep into *Ivanhoe* when he got the letter.

"I must go," he told Mama. "I shall leave the books for Nels and the children. Here is my check for all I owe you, madam, and my profound thanks for your hospitality."

We were sorry to see Mr. Hyde leave, but it was with great excitement that we brought his books out to the kitchen. There were so many of them! We read some of the titles: *A Tale of Two Cities, Nicholas Nickleby, Vanity Fair, The Adventures of Alice in Wonderland, Oliver Twist, A Midsummer Night's Dream*.

Mama dusted them reverently. "So much we can learn," she said. Nels, she added, could read aloud to us each evening, just as Mr. Hyde had done, because Nels too had a fine voice. I could see that made him very proud.

Mama showed Mr. Hyde's check to Aunt Jenny. "You see?" she said. "The warm coat I shall have after all."

It was too bad that Aunt Jenny was still there when Mr. Kruper came. Mr. Kruper owned the restaurant and bakery down the street and he was angry.

"That man Hyde was a crook!" he shouted. "Look at this check he gave me. It's no good!

The bank people tell me he cashed them all over the neighborhood."

Aunt Jenny's triumphant nod said as plainly as words — I told you so.

"I'll bet he owes you folks plenty too, eh?" Mr. Kruper asked.

Mama looked around at all of us. Her eyes rested longest on Nels. "Read," she told him gently, "read to us from *Ivanhoe*."

Then she walked to the stove and put the check into the flames.

"No," she answered Mr. Kruper. "No. He owes us nothing."

3 ਦ Mama
and the Hospital

Mama had tried everything she knew of to stop poor little Dagmar's earache. She'd warmed sweet oil and garlic, used the medicine Mr. Shultz had sent from the drugstore, but nothing had helped.

When Dr. Johnson came, he told Mama that Dagmar must be taken to the hospital.

"At once," he said. "We will have to operate."

I watched Mama's eyes grow dark with fright.

"Can wait?" she asked. "Until my husband comes home from work?"

"No time," the doctor said. "You must decide this morning. An immediate operation is her best chance."

Operation! Mama took a deep breath.

"We go," she said, and took down the Little Bank and emptied its contents onto the kitchen table. Then she looked up at the doctor. "Is enough?" she asked hopefully.

The doctor looked uncomfortable. "I was thinking of the county hospital," he explained.

"No," Mama said. "No. We pay."

"Well, then, take her to the clinic hospital."

"Clinic?"

"Yes. There you pay what you can afford," Dr. Johnson explained. "Your child will have the same care as the other patients."

Mama looked worried. "I — I do not understand so well."

"Just leave it to me, then. Dagmar will be well taken care of, I promise you. I myself will do the operation."

"Is so good of you," Mama said gratefully, and sent Nels for a blanket to wrap around Dagmar. And because Papa was at work, Nels and I went to the hospital with Mama.

When we got there, two nurses put Dagmar on a high table and started to wheel her down the hall. Mama tried to go along too.

"She is my little girl," Mama explained.

"Hospital rules," the nurse said firmly. "You must wait here."

Mama obediently let go of Dagmar's hand then, and walked with slow steps to the desk. They gave her papers to sign, but she didn't even try to read them. Her eyes kept looking down the hall.

Nels and I had never been in a hospital before. With great interest we watched ladies in blue and white uniforms and important-looking men with little black bags hurry in and out of doors; watched the cleaning women as they took mops and buckets and long-handled brooms out of the closet by the elevator.

"Dr. Johnson is *fine* doctor," Mama said suddenly. "Surely Dagmar will be all right."

I started to cry then, and Mama patted my shoulder, and told stories of the old country. But somehow, Mama didn't tell the stories as well as usual; she kept forgetting parts of them.

When Dr. Johnson came hurrying down the hall, Mama stood up quickly.

"Dagmar came through it fine," he told us. "She is sleeping now, from the anesthetic."

Mama smiled tremulously and shook hands twice with the doctor.

"I go to her now," she said happily.

Dr. Johnson coughed. "Sorry. Against clinic rules. See her tomorrow."

"But she is so *little*," Mama said. "When she wakes she will be frightened."

"The nurses will take excellent care of her. Don't worry. You see, for the first twenty-four hours, clinic patients are not allowed visitors. The wards must be kept quiet. No interruption of routine."

Mama didn't seem to understand. "I will not made a *sound*," she said.

Dr. Johnson looked at his watch, lifted his hat politely, and hurried out of the hospital.

Mama looked bewildered. "Come," she said to Nels and me. "Come. We go find Dagmar."

The nurse at the desk had quite a time explaining hospital rules to Mama.

"Your child is getting the best of care, madam," the lady kept repeating.

"Is *fine* hospital," Mama agreed. "I see her now?"

"*No* visitors for the first twenty-four hours, madam."

"Am *not* visitor," Mama explained patiently, "I am her Mama."

"*Against — the — rules!*" The nurse spoke loudly and slowly and with great finality.

Mama stood looking down the hall for such a long time that I had to touch her arm to remind her that Nels and I were still there.

She held my hand tightly as we walked to the streetcar and never said a word all the way home.

Christine had kept lunch hot for us, but Mama just drank two cups of coffee. She did not take off her hat.

"We must think of some way," she worried, and we children sat very still.

"They'll let you see Dagmar tomorrow," Nels reminded her. "They said so."

"But unless I see her today," Mama asked, "how will I know that all is well with her? What can I tell Papa when he comes home from work?"

15

She shook her head. "No. *Today* I see Dagmar."

She stood up suddenly and took paper and string out of the kitchen drawer. Carefully, she wrapped Dagmar's little doll in one neat package and our big picture book in another. We watched uneasily.

"It will be like this," Mama explained. "I will go past the hospital desk very quickly. If anyone asks where I go, I will just say, 'Delivering packages to Dagmar.' "

When Mama came back — still carrying the packages — we knew she'd been unsuccessful. We knew too that she was upset, because she answered us in Norwegian.

"Almost," she said wearily, "almost did I get down the hall."

Then she tied the big apron around her waist, filled the bucket with hot, soapy water, and started to scrub the kitchen floor.

"You scrubbed yesterday," Christine reminded her.

"And the floor isn't a speck dirty," I said.

"It's almost time to get dinner," Nels protested.

"Comes a time," Mama answered strangely, "when you must get down on your knees."

And the whiteness of her face made me want to cry again.

Mama had scrubbed all but the part near

the back door when she stood up suddenly and handed the scrub brush to Christine.

"You finish the floor. Katrin, you come with me." And she sent me for my coat.

"Come where, Mama?"

"To the hospital." Her face was serene. "I have thought of way to see Dagmar sure."

We walked in so quietly that the nurse at the desk didn't even look up. Mama motioned for me to sit in the big chair by the door. While I watched — mouth open in surprise — Mama took off her hat and coat and gave them to me to hold. Only then did I notice that she'd kept her apron on. She tiptoed over to the big closet by the elevator and took out a damp mop. She pushed the mop past the desk and as the nurse looked up, Mama nodded brightly.

"Very dirty floors," Mama said.

"Yes. I'm glad they've finally decided to clean them," the nurse answered. She looked at Mama curiously. "Aren't you working late?"

Mama just pushed more vigorously, each swipe of the mop taking her farther and farther down the hall. I watched until she was out of sight and the nurse had turned back to writing in the big book. Then I saw that I had held Mama's hat so tightly, one side was all out of shape.

After a long time, Mama came back. Her eyes were shining.

While the nurse stared with amazement, Mama placed the mop neatly back in the closet, put on her hat and coat, and took my hand. As we turned to go out the door, Mama bowed politely to the nurse and said, "Thank you."

Outside, Mama told me: "Dagmar is fine. No fever. I felt her forehead."

"You *saw* her, Mama?"

"Of course. She wakened while I was with her. I told her about clinic rules, she will not expect us until tomorrow."

"You won't try to see her again," I asked, "before then?"

"Why," Mama said, "that would be against the rules. Besides, I have seen for myself that all goes well with her. Papa will not worry, now."

I swallowed hard.

"Is a *fine* hospital," Mama said happily. Then she clicked her tongue disapprovingly. "But such floors! A mop is never good. Floors should be scrubbed with a brush."

4 ❧ *Mama's Uncle Chris*

Papa called Mama's Uncle Chris a "black Norwegian" — because of his singular swarthiness and dark mustache; but there were others in the family who maintained that old Uncle Chris was "black" in a different way. Notably in his heart.

He was a giant of a man, my Great-uncle Chris, and his voice was a bellow. I never knew him to move slowly, and whenever he limped furiously through our house, we children scattered.

When the Aunts were together and their bachelor Uncle's name was mentioned, they would begin to cluck disapprovingly. Strange tales would be told of his disturbing secretiveness, dark hints dropped; and the smaller children would be sent out of the room.

For one thing, Uncle Chris was head of the family, and he never allowed them to forget it. Grown women though the Aunts might be, he treated them always as if they were stupid children.

Except Mama. To her he gave a certain

grudging approval. Because, Aunt Jenny said, she was the youngest. But Papa thought it was because Mama was the only one of the sisters to resemble Uncle Chris's mother, who died when he was small.

Then too Mama was the only one who ever spoke up for Uncle Chris. "He walks ever with pain," she would excuse him.

"Nonsense!" the Aunts said. Oh, true it was, they conceded, that Uncle Chris limped — because of that accident in the old country. But had anyone ever heard him complain of pain? No, she need not waste any sympathy they told Mama; he was just downright mean. Blackhearted, that Chris.

Ah, but the Aunts were brave when they discussed their absent Uncle. When he was there, fuming with his great impatience, roaring at them, scolding them — it was a different story. It was a meek "Yes, Uncle Chris. No, Uncle Chris. You are right, Uncle Chris."

Papa said it was a good thing for the Aunts that Uncle Chris came to the city only a few times a year. The rest of the time he roamed up and down the state, buying old and run-down farms. These he would work furiously, bully back to productivity, and then sell.

"At a handsome profit, never doubt," Aunt Jenny said.

And the Aunts would speculate anew as to *what* Uncle Chris did with all his money.

We never knew just when Uncle Chris would descend upon us. One moment everything would be peaceful and quiet; then, without warning, there would be a stamping and a roaring and we knew that he was back in town.

We children would have to line up for inspection, and Uncle Chris's blue eyes, startlingly light against the blackness of his brows, would glare at us. Like as not, he would thump us sharply between our shoulder blades. "Stand tall!" he would command. Then, "You brush your teet' *good*?"

We would nod timidly.

"Oranges!" he would shout at Mama. "Gif dem more oranges!"

Grumbling and snorting, he would go down to the wholesale district and send us up boxes of oranges.

"Sour old things," Aunt Marta would complain. "What good are oranges?"

Mama didn't know, but we children had to eat them.

Oranges, Aunt Sigrid said, were the only things Uncle Chris ever gave away, he was that stingy.

Aunt Jenny guessed he needed his money for other purposes. "Bottles," she hinted darkly. And we children were able to add another piece to the fascinating puzzle that was Uncle Chris.

21

Uncle Chris DRANK.

He had done other terrible things too. Just take, for example, the matter of the family's two cherished heirlooms: Great-great-grandma's carved bridal chest and the Viking drinking horn. Hadn't Uncle Chris, without consulting anyone, gone ahead and *sold* them?

When the Aunts reproached him timidly, he'd glared.

"In your veins runs de blood of de Kings of Norvay!" he had shouted. "What need haf you of heirlooms?"

And he never would tell what he did with the money.

Take too the matter of Aunt Trina's dowry.

Trina was our maiden Aunt, and the family had despaired of ever getting her married. Then she met Mr. Thirkelsen. He was a small and extremely timid gentleman, and old Uncle Chris nearly frightened him out of his wits. Uncle Chris thundered question after question at poor Mr. Thirkelsen, demanding to know in detail all about his family, his financial status, and his intentions toward Trina.

And no sooner had Mr. Thirkelsen weathered that storm and got his breath back then Uncle Chris took him out to the kitchen and talked him right out of Aunt Trina's dowry money!

It was a miracle, the Aunts said later, that they finally got Trina married.

But the very blackest thing Uncle Chris ever did was to Aunt Marta, and we thought she would never forgive him. Marta's youngest boy, my cousin Arne, had fallen off a coal wagon and injured his knee against the cobblestones. Although Aunt Marta poulticed it carefully, the swelling didn't go down. We noticed that Arne favored the knee as he walked, that he complained sometimes of its hurting him, but Aunt Marta said there was nothing to worry about.

But Uncle Chris thought differently. When he saw the queer lump on Arne's knee, he shouted with rage. And before we knew it, he had Arne in a hospital and in a plaster cast! All this, mind you, without once consulting Aunt Marta or her husband.

Uncle Chris's highhandedness, Aunt Marta said, had gone just too far this time. To put a child of Arne's age through such unnecessary pain! Hadn't she raised four children, she demanded of the Aunts? Didn't he think a mother knew anything?

But Uncle Chris just glared at everyone and said: "Vomen! Phh!"

Arne told me about the hospital later. He said that when the pain was at its very worst, there in the beginning, Uncle Chris had shouted at him: "Arne! Don't you know any svear vords?"

Arne said he was so shocked that he stopped

crying. (And that all he could think of was the big bar of brown laundry soap his mother had at home.)

When he shook his head, Uncle Chris said: "I vill tell you two fine ones to use ven de pain is bad."

And he did.

Arne said that they helped.

"Nights, when I couldn't sleep," Arne told me in a whisper, "Uncle Chris sat by my bed and sang songs to me. Soft, in Norwegian."

I was shocked beyond words. Uncle Chris *singing*?

"Arne! You must have been dreaming!"

Arne shook his head stubbornly. "He sang."

Neither of us ever told, though. We knew the Aunts wouldn't believe us.

Uncle Chris was gone for a long time after that. When next we heard, he was on a farm in one of the valley towns, and very ill. Dying, the letter said.

Aunt Jenny wouldn't believe it. According to her, Uncle Chris was too mean to die.

"The wages of sin," Aunt Marta said.

"Oh, no!" Mama protested. "He is old. It is perhaps time for him to go."

Aunt Trina fluttered that everyone must be brave, and while she did not like to mention such a matter at a time like this, when they divided Uncle Chris's estate would the Aunts please remember that there was her dowry money to be paid back first?

Uncle Chris's neighbor met us at the train and took us out to the farm. Our manner was decorous and quiet, but before we reached the front door we could hear Uncle Chris shouting — for a drink of whisky.

Mama looked stricken, but she marched into his room and took his big hand in hers.

"Uncle Chris," she scolded gently, "that will not help now."

He looked at her for a long time, his great head moving restlessly against the pillow. "Lille ven," he said — which means "Little friend" in Norwegian — "Lille ven, I must not die. Is yet so much to — " Then he seemed to notice the Aunts there at the foot of the bed.

"You tink I am afraid to die?" he raged at them. He sat right up and roared. "Get out! Get out!"

And as I scurried after them, I heard him say to Mama, "Vomen! Vomen! Phh!"

We sat in the dusty, old-fashioned parlor, waiting. At last Mama came out. "Uncle Chris is — gone," she said, and put her head down on Papa's shoulder.

Aunt Trina cleared her throat several times. Mama looked up and held out a grimy, faded notebook.

"Ah," Aunt Trina sighed. "Ah, his will."

Mama shook her head. "There is no money left."

There was a shocked silence. Aunt Trina wept into her handkerchief and mourned her dowry money. Aunt Sigrid spoke of Viking horns and bridal chests, while Aunt Jenny muttered, "Bottles!"

"Not so!" Mama cried. "Uncle Chris wrote it all down — how he spent the money. Here," she handed the notebook to me, "read it. Out loud."

I had a hard time deciphering the cramped, smudged handwriting. There was a name and an amount at the head of each page.

"Joseph Spinelli," I read. "Four yrs old. Tubercular left leg. $237.00. Walks."

I turned the page. "Jaimie Kelly. Nine yrs. Curvature. $433.00. Walks."

One after the other, I read the items.

"Esta Jensen. Eleven yrs. Braces. $121.00."

"Sam Bernstein. Five yrs. Clubfoot. $452.16. Walks."

There were more names, but my throat had tightened so that I could not read on.

Mama looked pleadingly at the Aunts. "It was good," she said firmly. But she also seemed to be asking a question of them.

Aunt Sigrid stood up and took off her coat. "There is work to be done," was all she said.

Aunt Trina put her handkerchief into her

purse and offered to make coffee for everyone. Aunt Marta looked at Arne.

"It was *good*," Mama insisted again.

Aunt Jenny, who was the oldest, touched Mama's hand briefly. "It was good," she agreed.

And all the Aunts nodded briskly.

5 ❧ Mama
and the Big City

In those days, if anyone had asked Mama un-expectedly, "What nationality are you?" I be-lieve she would have answered without hesita-tion, "I am a San Franciscan."

Then quickly, lest you tease her, she would add, "I mean Norvegian. American citizen."

But her first statement would be the true one.

Because from the moment she was to step off the ferryboat, confused and lonely in a strange land, San Francisco was to become sud-denly and uniquely her own.

"Is like Norvay," the Aunts said Mama had declared.

And straightway she'd taken the city to her heart.

Mama learned so many things about San Francisco. She could tell you how to get to Telegraph Hill; what time the boats came in at Fisherman's Wharf; the names of the young boys who tended the steaming crab kettles

28

along Bay Street; and where to find the blue and yellow lupins at Land's End.

The cable cars were an endless delight, and Mama's idea of a perfect Sunday afternoon was for Papa to take us riding on them from one transfer point to another.

Papa would tell of the time Mama took out her citizenship papers and astounded the solemn court by suddenly reciting the names of the streets. "Turk, Eddy, Ellis, O'Farrell," Mama had said proudly, "Geary, Post, Sutter, Bush, and Pine."

Papa said the clerk had quite a time making Mama understand that such knowledge was not necessary for citizenship.

Mama made friends with an Armenian lady who had a store out on Third Street, and gave her her best lutefisk recipe. Best of all though, Mama liked to explore Chinatown. Old Sing Fat and Mama held long conversations over the counters of his Grant Avenue Bazaar. Like as not she would come home to Castro Street with a tiny bag of lichee nuts or preserved ginger. And if any of us were ill in bed, Mama would go down and get us a small package of those Chinese water flowers that open into amazing beauty when dropped into water.

And if anyone ever asked us where we were born, Mama instructed us, we should say "San Francisco." Didn't copies of our birth certificates, neatly framed and hung on the wall of

Papa's and Mama's room, testify to that proud fact?

"After all," Papa used to tease her, "after all, San Francisco isn't the *world*."

But to Mama it was just that. The world.

Papa had been working steadily for a long time now, and for once we had a little money ahead. And Mama had told us that within a few months there would be a new brother or sister.

Then a real estate salesman got hold of Papa and tried to sell him a chicken ranch across the Bay.

Just a little money down, the salesman said, and Papa could pay off the balance like rent. And just think, he told us, there were also five whole acres of fruit trees.

"Sunshine!" the man said enthusiastically. "No fog."

Mama bridled as if someone had said something against one of her children.

"Fog is good," she declared. "Is healthy."

"But there will be eggs for the little ones," he countered. "And plenty of milk."

"There is a cow?" Papa asked.

Well, no, the salesman admitted, no cow. But there were four fine goats.

I saw Mama wrinkle her nose.

Only after Papa said that it would be nice to be your own boss and have a place of your own, instead of being a carpenter — only after we children and Nels had coaxed and pleaded — did Mama reluctantly agree to the move across the Bay.

It was fun at first, helping Papa to prune the trees and to mend the roof of the sagging little house; fun to carry the water from the well and to chop the wood. I remember what a great time Nels had whitewashing the chicken coop. Dagmar helped Mama start a little vegetable garden, and Christine and I took turns milking the ever-present goats.

But when the cold weather came, our enthusiasm for country life waned rapidly. We children were not used to tumbling sleepily out of bed while it was still dark, eating our breakfast by lamplight, then trudging miles to school.

Nor were we used to a one-room schoolhouse, to playmates who called us "Scandahoovians." Ours had been a more cosmopolitan atmosphere.

"Hicks!" Christine and I retaliated sulkily. "Country hicks!" And knew a deep homesickness.

Dagmar mourned the merry-go-round and the ponies at the park, while Nels spoke often and wistfully of the big city library with its thousands of books.

Christine and I missed the sidewalks. Our

beloved roller skates hung idly in the closet, and as we oiled them carefully every Saturday morning, we remembered that once we had been the very best skaters on the block.

Only Mama never complained. But we saw her stand for long moments at the window — looking westward.

Papa worked early and late, but fought a losing battle. We watched the young trees in the orchard, our carefully tended garden, shrivel and blacken with frost. We had not had money enough to provide smudge pots.

The chickens came down with a strange and baffling illness; most of them died and the few surviving hens stopped laying eggs.

Only the goats kept producing. Our pantry shelves were stocked with the brown goat cheese Mama had made.

For the first Christmas in our lives, we children did not get to see the big city stores and the wonderful window displays. And Papa's toolbox was packed away in the closet with our skates.

On New Year's Eve we were allowed to stay up. Mama made "sweet soup" for us, and she and Papa said Skoal! and wished us each a Godt Nytaar as they drank their coffee.

At midnight Mama held up her hand. "Listen!" she said.

We couldn't hear anything.

"Bells!" Mama said. "Bells and whistles in San Francisco."

Papa looked worried. "Is too far to hear," he told her gently. "You imagine things."

I thought I saw tears in Mama's eyes, but I must have been mistaken. Mama never cried.

"It is not good," Papa said heavily, "for carpenter to try to be farmer."

"Such talk!" Mama protested. But Papa's shoulders did not straighten. And the next day he went to see the real estate salesman. But the man didn't seem interested in us anymore. So then Papa had Nels write out an advertisement for the newspaper. But even that wasn't successful.

We only had one answer, an old couple by the name of Sonderman. They liked the chicken ranch, but as Mr. Sonderman explained, they had their big house on Steiner Street to dispose of first.

"Eleven rooms," Mrs. Sonderman told us, "and since our boys are grown and gone away, Mr. Sonderman and I just rattle around in it."

Of course eleven rooms was too big for us, and never in the world could we get enough money together to put a down payment on it — even counting what Papa had in the chicken ranch.

But Mama never seemed to know when something was hopeless. She made several trips

over to the city to see the Steiner Street house
and to talk with the Sondermans.

Then Aunt Jenny came over to see us.

"To visit for a while," she said brightly. And
we children were much too polite to tell her
we knew she'd come to stay with us until after
our new baby was born.

Mama made fresh coffee and she and Aunt
Jenny and Papa sat down to the kitchen table.

"What is wrong with the children?" Aunt
Jenny demanded.

Mama's eyes were worried as she looked at
each of us.

"They do not look good?" she asked anxiously.

"Such long faces they have," Aunt Jenny explained.

Mama looked at us again. "I see what you
mean," she said slowly. "They have not happiness."

Aunt Jenny told us news of the old neighborhood. We remembered the Andersons?
Well, they had moved over to Castro Street.

And Peter Larson, Anna Lundquist's brother, had got the carpenter contract on the new
high school, and he had told Aunt Jenny he
just wished he had Papa for a carpenter fore-
man.

Papa held out his earth-stained hands.
"Would be good," he sighed, "to hold tools
again. To smell the fresh new wood."

Mama stood up suddenly. "I just think," she said. "That Sonderman house — eleven rooms. Jenny, that would make a fine boardinghouse."

Aunt Jenny laughed shortly. "Indeed. And where would you find time — *now* — to do the work?"

Mama's face reddened. "But *after* — Papa, the children — all would help. We would work together."

Absolute nonsense, Aunt Jenny declared. Besides, she pointed out, we had only about four rooms of furniture.

"But we could get more, Jenny. With Papa working for Peter Larson."

Aunt Jenny shook her head as if the whole plan was hopeless.

"I think," Mama said stubbornly, "that the Sondermans would be willing to give us three — maybe four — months' rent on the Steiner house for what we have paid on this place. Mrs. Sonderman *likes* chicken farm."

Papa laughed out loud for the first time in months. "And goats," he said. "Old Mr. Sonderman likes goats."

Mama and Papa looked at each other for a long time. Then Papa went down the road to phone. When he came back he nodded his head and said, "Four months' free rent." And he brought his tool chest out of the closet and started sharpening the tools.

"We go," Mama said happily, "we go." And sent Nels for boxes.

"Wait," Aunt Jenny pleaded. "Wait and talk this over. You should think a long time before you make a move like this."

"We go," Mama said again. "We go today." She started taking the dishes off the shelves.

Aunt Jenny choked on her coffee. "Such foolishness! You can't. You must wait until after — "

There was a strange urgency in Mama's voice. "We go *today*. The house is vacant. The Sondermans moved their things over to their married son's last week."

"And what of all your hard work here?" Aunt Jenny demanded. "What have you got out of it?"

"Four months' free rent in a big house in San Francisco," Mama said. "And goat cheese." She pointed to the pantry shelves. "*Lots* of goat cheese." And Mama was smiling.

Late that afternoon, when Papa had brought the last box into what had been the Sondermans' house and was now ours, Mama told Nels he could go to the library, and she sent us children out to play.

Eagerly and joyously we skated up and down the block, exploring the new neighborhood, making plans for the next day.

36

When it grew dark, we went home for dinner and found that all the Aunts were there. It was Aunt Jenny, however, who told us the news. She looked as if someone had played a trick on her.

"You have a new baby sister," she told us grimly, and took us down the hall to the room that was now Papa's and Mama's.

Mama smiled reassuringly at us as we tiptoed in. She lifted the blanket from the tiny bundle on her arm. "Her name is Kaaren," she said.

Papa turned to beam at us and we saw that he was hanging our framed birth certificates in a neat row against the wall. He took a tack out of his mouth.

Aunt Sigrid came in with soup for Mama. "Say," she said, "isn't it funny how all your children are born in San Francisco?"

"Funny?" Aunt Jenny demanded crossly. "*Funny?*"

"Is good," Mama said happily, "is good."

6 &~ Mama
and Her Little Ladies

It was like starting a new life — living in the big house on Steiner Street. Never before had the family had an upstairs, a downstairs, a basement, and an attic. In addition to the big high-ceilinged rooms there were two long halls, an enormous kitchen, and a back porch that Papa intended to close in.

Even Aunt Jenny finally had to concede that the Steiner Street house would make a fine boardinghouse. Mama's plans for furnishing it were simple. We had enough furniture for four rooms; we would live in three rooms and rent the other. When we had made enough money from our first boarder, we would furnish another room and have a second boarder — and so on, until all the rooms were rented.

Mama was very proud of her figuring.

And at this time I became very interested in myself. I seemed to come into focus as the other figures of the family moved into the background. I became **Kathryn** (spelled with a "y") and Katrin only at home.

The nearest school was Winford, one of the few public schools for girls. Mrs. Karboe, our new and very helpful neighbor, was so *glad* that we were going to have the *privilege* of attending it.

"Such a *wonderful* school," she said. "Winford has a *splendid* reputation! Turns out *regular little ladies*."

Mrs. Karboe had a fascinating habit of accenting her words.

She had been a *teacher* once, she told us, and she *knew* about such things.

We could see that it made Mama very happy that her girls were going to be turned into little ladies.

"Sissies," I muttered to Christine, but she didn't respond.

Evidently, the idea of a girls' school appealed to her. While I — well of course it was out of the question to come right out and say that you liked boys — liked them when they let you play on their team or helped you out with silly arithmetic problems — and it was probably very *un*ladylike, but it was my personal opinion that boys in a schoolroom gave it a certain interest.

I was, however, philosophical. I would probably like Winford very much. My grades were always good, I had skipped twice. And it might be fun to go to a school that was, according to Mrs. Karboe, so "*tony.*"

Because Mama was so busy with our new baby, and because I was the oldest girl, I was entrusted with the task of enrolling Dagmar and taking care of Christine's transfer and my own. Scrubbed and braided and shining, we started out on Monday morning.

Miss Grimes, Winford's principal, was tall and thin and had beautiful white hair that coiled intricately upon the top of her head. Her pompadour rose to an incredible height, and I found myself counting the little sausage curls that marched up both sides and down the back. She wore a high-collared shirtwaist and a sweeping black skirt. The chain of her glasses disappeared into a round gold box she wore on her chest, and I was fascinated with the way it worked.

"*Ladies* do not stare!" were Miss Grimes's first words to me, and she did not seem at all happy to get three brand-new pupils.

"Oh," she said without enthusiasm, when I told her our names. "Oh. Swedish."

"No, ma'am, if you please. *Norwegian.*"

Miss Grimes shrugged. "Swedish, Norwegian — it's all the same."

"Oh, *no*, ma'am!"

The outraged look on her face stopped my earnest protest.

40

"*Ladies*," she snapped, "do not contradict their elders. *I* say they are all the same."

Right then and there I lost all faith in Miss Grimes. She might be very highly educated, as Mrs. Karboe had said, but for her not to know that Norwegians were very different from Swedes! She should have heard my old Uncle Chris on the subject. "*Svedes?*" I could hear him roar, "Svedes? Vat are Svedes but Norvegians vit der brains knocked out?"

Another lady came into the principal's office. She too was tall and thin and wore shirtwaist and skirt, but her smile was kind.

"Miss Lyons," Miss Grimes said unhappily, "we have three new pupils."

"How nice," Miss Lyons said. "Three newcomers to the Halls of Learning."

"Halls of Learning indeed," Miss Grimes sniffed. "To the melting pot, you mean. I don't know what Winford's coming to. The Vanetti girl, and the Gubbenstein creature, and now three towheaded Swedes."

"Norwegians," I said, but in a small whisper.

"In all my years as principal of Winford," Miss Grimes complained, "it's never been as bad as this. Why, I can remember when only girls from the *finest* families came here. Next thing you know," she prophesied darkly, "we'll be getting Negroes, or even—" her voice faltered, "or even—*Orientals*."

41

I held tightly to Dagmar's hand and was suddenly, passionately grateful that I was not an Oriental girl. I stole a glance at Christine. She was gazing calmly out the window, the usual serene and withdrawn look upon her face. And for the hundredth time, I envied her her detachment.

Miss Grimes wrote our names down in a big book. "Dagmar to the first grade," she said wearily. "Christine — what outlandish names they give their children — Christine to Miss Donner's room, and the oldest one there to Miss Scanlon."

I helped Miss Lyons deliver Christine and Dagmar to their respective rooms, and then reluctantly opened the door that was marked: "Miss Scanlon. Grade 8-A."

The room seemed full of girls, full of eyes that watched my every move. As I advanced toward Miss Scanlon's desk, the squeak of my newly soled shoes was loud in the silence. Somebody giggled, and I felt the beginning of the blush that was the bane of my life.

I held out the slip of paper that was my transfer, dropped it, retrieved it, and dropped it again. By the time I succeeded in getting it into Miss Scanlon's hand, the room was loud with laughter.

"Girls," Miss Scanlon chided. "Girls!"

She motioned me to a desk in the rear of the

room and I scuttled toward it as if it were sanctuary.

"Although it *is* unusual," Miss Scanlon lectured, "to have new pupils enter this grade — because, of course, most of our girls have been with us from the first — we must not forget that we are *la-dies*."

I blushed more furiously (if that were possible), and felt guilty, as if I had made them break some sacred tradition.

My new schoolmates were not a friendly lot. Only the little dark girl across the aisle smiled at me. At the first recess, she walked over to me.

"My name is Carmelita Vanetti," she said. "I'm new too."

I was humbly grateful for her notice.

"Don't pay any attention to the girls in our room," she comforted me. "They're a stuck-up bunch."

"Oh," I said. "Oh."

"They're *cliquey*," she whispered fiercely, and I nodded, though I hadn't the least idea what "cliquey" meant.

I did know that they were better dressed than I. That they whispered and giggled when I came close to them.

"Hester Prinn and Madeline Cartright run the whole class," Carmelita continued, "and silly Miss Scanlon too. Hester's mother, if you please, is a 'Winford Girl' and came here to Miss Grimes years ago. And Madeline's father is some big politician."

"Oh," I said again. "Oh."

As we filed back to class I said to myself that Carmelita must be mistaken. The girls acted strangely because it was my first day. Later on, when they got to know me, they would be different. Always people had been friendly toward me.

The unfortunate day dragged to a close. There was one bright moment when I was the only one in the class to know the birthplace of Lorenzo the Magnificent, and another when I knew the chief exports of Russia.

Then, just as we were putting away books and pens and two of the girls had been appointed eraser monitors, Dagmar sidled timidly into the room. Looking around, she queried softly: "Christine? Katrin? I have to go home."

I tried to catch Dagmar's attention, but Miss Scanlon had swooped down. "Oh, you little Precious," she gurgled. "Look, girls, isn't she a Precious?"

"Yes, Miss Scanlon," they chorused obediently.

"Please," I waved my hand wildly, "please, Miss Scanlon — "

"You stay in your seat until dismissal," Miss

Scanlon said sharply. Then: "And what is your name?" she crooned to Dagmar.

"My name is Dagmar. And I have to go *home*."

"I think I'll steal you," Miss Scanlon teased, "and keep you here with us."

Dagmar squirmed restlessly. "Katrin?" she begged. "Where is Katrin?"

"Oh, you mean Kathryn. Say *Kathryn*, Precious, *th, th*."

I was cold with a sudden suspicion and rushed to the front of the room. "Please, Miss Scanlon, let her go. This is her very first day at school and I don't think she knows — "

But Miss Scanlon had tightened her hold. "Not until," she said kindly but firmly, "not until she shows Miss Scanlon that she can say your name correctly."

"Oh, Katrin, I have to go *home*," Dagmar wailed urgently.

"Say *Kathryn*," Miss Scanlon persisted. "Like this," — she put her tongue between her teeth — "th, th, *th*."

"They call me Katrin at home," I whispered fiercely, "it is the Norwegian — "

"Ah, but we are going to learn the American way," said Miss Scanlon archly. "Aren't we, Precious?"

But Precious had succumbed to a need that was the same in any language and, with stricken eyes, I watched catastrophe overtake poor little Dagmar.

Miss Scanlon stepped back in a hurry. "You *nasty* little girl," she snapped.

Tearfully, Dagmar looked down at the widening pool at her feet. "I *told* you," she sobbed, "that I had to go home."

The room hissed with shocked expressions and I knew that my foolish dream of friendliness from these girls was finished.

"She didn't know," I said numbly. "She is so tiny — this is her first day — "

"Go," Miss Scanlon said with icy dignity, "go and find the janitress — and a mop."

Hand in hand, and with broken hearts, Dagmar and I left the room.

Christine waited for us at the end of the hall. We told her what had happened.

"Mama's Little Ladies," was all she said. "Mama's Little Ladies."

7 ?? *Mama*
and the Higher Culture

We had our first boarder in the new house. Her name was Miss Durant, and she was a telephone operator who worked at night. We saw very little of her. At first, we children had understood that our new boarder was a man; we thought the name was "Mister Ann." And the first time Dagmar had seen her, she'd run crying to Mama that a strange lady had a key to our front door. Miss Durant didn't seem to mind the flurry though. She was a tiny, quiet person who kept very much to her own room, the big front bedroom upstairs. Mama worried about Miss Durant because Miss Durant insisted upon all her vegetables being served raw — even the potatoes — and she wouldn't even taste the rich nourishing soups Mama tried to tempt her with. Papa joked that the first big wind would blow her away and rob us of our first boarder.

Miss Durant was a great reader though. Her room was piled with magazines, and once she gave me a box of them to throw away. She had put string around the box, but instead of throwing the magazines away, I'd taken them up to my attic.

The family still hadn't got used to the big house. Mama loved the spacious kitchen and the large dining room. She and Papa had got a dining-room table that had six leaves in it, and when it was opened out it would seat twenty people. And every Saturday, we'd go down to the secondhand stores on McAllister Street and pick up chairs. Mama had her eye on a big brass bedstead and a carpet, and soon now we'd have another room furnished, and then we would get a couple more boarders.

There was a cubbyhole underneath the stairs, right off the first-floor hall. This Christine usurped and decorated with her three burst-leather cushions, Aunt Sigrid's discarded bead portières, Uncle Chris's old Morris chair, and the brown jardinière that had got broken in the moving. She called her cubbyhole her "bood-war," and wouldn't let any of us in without a special invitation. Aunt Jenny said that "bood-war" had a — well, a "fast" sound, but that only made Christine more stubborn, and she wouldn't call it anything else.

Not to be outdone, I took over the attic. It was much too big and draughty to be made into any cozy bood-war, so I called it my "study," and loved every foot of its bareness. I jeered at Christine's bead portières and boasted that *my* attic had a *door* and a *key* that locked. (It locked if you had a pair of pliers to help turn the rusty mechanism.)

Possession of the attic made up, to some extent, for the misery of being alternately ignored and taunted by my schoolmates at Winford. For the very first time in my life I had a place all my own. And for the first time in my life I heard rain falling directly onto a roof. My attic skylight could be lifted up and held in place with a heavy piece of firewood. I would perch precariously on the sill and dream long dreams.

I would contemplate the rusty drainpipe that ascended the gloomy Karboe house next door. Only of course it wasn't a drainpipe, it was a trellis of ivy — and by such means would the young prince come to rescue the beautiful young princess held captive in the high tower.

I could gaze into our dreary empty backyard. Then the red geraniums that Mama had set out would become rare, exotic blossoms — and I could see a great white charger pawing at the broken pieces of pavement.

"Romeo — ah, Romeo!" I would whisper dramatically.

Sometimes Romeo would remain stubbornly silent. Or I would get tired of saying his lines for him. So then I would put the skylight back into place, bar the door, and read the vivid magazines that Miss Durant had given me to throw away. I had hidden them in the dusty niche formed by the floor joists.

I don't know what impulse made me hide them. Perhaps I knew that Mama would not approve of the brilliantly colored frontispieces. Especially the one that showed a leering individual busily engaged in choking a golden-haired lady. I knew quite well that Mama would not appreciate my favorite: the one where the terrible-looking Chinaman was about to plunge a curved dagger into the throat of his equally sinister-looking countryman.

The stories within were the most exciting I had ever read. Even the advertisements were good. I wasn't particularly interested in the one that offered to Take Away the Curse of the Childless Home; nor had I a boss I wanted to impress with my sudden knowledge of Accountancy. The one that showed the big man in the tiger skin intrigued me briefly, and I toyed with the idea of suddenly acquiring bulging muscles and becoming the Strong Man of my neighborhood. But I discarded that thought the moment I saw the following advertisement:

"DO YOU WANT TO BECOME A WRITER?" it asked in large clear type. And continued: "WRITING SECRETS. This Complete Course in Motion Picture, Novel, Short Story, Poetry,

Drama, Pageantry, and Newspaper Technique yours for only $7.00! USED BY ALL FAMOUS AUTHORS."

Why, how *wonderful,* I thought. So that's how it was done? If one only had seven dollars one could become a Famous Author overnight. Think of the money one could make! Money for Mama, for Papa, for Nels. Why, we could even go right down to one of the big furniture stores and order brand-new furniture for all the rooms. All at one time! For that matter, Mama wouldn't have to run a boardinghouse anymore. With all the money that I could make, none of the family would have to do any work at all.

And oh, wouldn't Aunt Jenny be jealous? All the Aunts, in fact. The next time they brought a box of clothes to us, I could say gaily: "Oh, but my goodness, we don't need any clothes. It is very kind of you, I'm sure" (I'd have to be polite, on account of Mama), "but just come see our new coats. Yes, they all have fur on the collars. Will you take a ride with us in our new automobile? And you won't mind if we stop at the Bank, will you? I simply cannot carry all this money around with me."

And at school, Miss Scanlon would tap on her desk with her pencil. "Girls," she would say. "Girls, we have a Famous Author in our midst. Stand up, Kathryn."

51

And the girls would clap, and they would quarrel among themselves as to which one would walk with me at recess. And I would make Hester and Madeline take Carmelita Vanetti into the "clique" along with me. Miss Grimes would probably brag to the Board of Education about me, and would call me lovingly "a Winford Girl."

I sighed. It could all come true too, if by some miracle I could just get this magic course. But with only seventeen cents —

Something about the finer print caught my eye. "Yours for five days' free trial," it said. "If you are not satisfied with the course at the end of five days, return at absolutely no cost to yourself."

My goodness! Here was golden opportunity. With trembling hands, I clipped the coupon and got out the fancy letter paper Aunt Trina had given me the Christmas before.

I tried hard to make the letter sound grown-up and Famous Authorish.

"I have had," I wrote, "some success with my Writing Endeavors." (Well, I silenced my conscience, hadn't I always had an A in composition?) "But now," I continued, "I wish to turn to the Broader Fields of Motion Picture, Novels, and Drama."

I signed it with a "Mrs." in front of my name. Surely that would make them think I was grown-up.

Two of my precious seventeen cents went for a stamp. The rest I invested in the largest notebook I could find. Five days were, after all, only five days, and I would have to copy the precious secrets in a hurry.

I planned to keep a bowl of warm water by my side as I wrote, so that I could bathe my aching fingers. Wasn't that what Mr. Edgar Allan Poe did when his hands got cramped from writing? I was willing — nay, anxious — to suffer for my art.

The days winged by. School was no longer a torture. I could stand being ignored for a little while.

"Just you wait," I told Carmelita mysteriously. "Just you wait. They'll be glad to have us for friends very soon now."

No longer did Mama have to call me three times before I tumbled reluctantly out of bed. I was the first one up in the morning now, and I haunted the front steps, watching for the mailman.

"Something is wrong with you, Katrin?" Mama looked worried.

"Oh, *no*, Mama."

In my heart, I knew that Mama would not approve of what I had done. She would think that sending for the course without planning to pay for it would be dishonest. To copy off the precious secrets and then send the course back — that would be cheating. I couldn't see that it was any different from going down to the big department stores and saying to the saleslady, "I'm just looking, thank you." That's what Aunt Jenny did all the time.

I badgered the poor postman mercilessly. "*When* would I get my package?" He was so kind. He figured it all out for me on the back of an envelope. Six days going — six days coming — say two days for a little leeway — well, twelve days would be his guess.

I thanked him effusively. And it was *so* important, I told him, that the package be delivered in the morning. Since in the afternoons I had to be in school, and since I didn't want the family to know — "It's a sort of present," I said, "for them all. A big surprise."

The postman nodded understandingly and assured me that the important package would be delivered to me personally, and in the morning.

Ah, but he was a most superior postman. I would, I promised myself, buy him a grand present out of my first big check. Perhaps — yes, a gold watch and chain.

But the postman's twelve days stretched to fifteen, to twenty, and still the eagerly awaited package failed to arrive. Sadly, I concluded that the people in New York were smarter than I'd thought and they hadn't been taken in by my grown-upness at all; not even by that "Mrs." in front of my name.

Maybe I'd have to change my daydreams around to include a rich husband. I could have him handsome, like Mr. William Hart, but it was a nuisance to have to wait to grow up. I wanted that money *now*.

Then, just as I was ready to give up hope — to relinquish my great riches — the package arrived. Mama had taken Baby Kaaren and gone over to Aunt Jenny's, and I was alone with my joy. I dashed up to my attic, my heart thudding with anticipation. With fumbling nervous fingers, I opened the package. My Open Sesame to Success!

There were seven gray little pamphlets.

Eagerly I skimmed through them, hunting frantically for the Secret Technique of Famous Authors. But alas, the long, involved paragraphs were difficult to understand; the print was small and faded, and the text abounded with unfamiliar words.

I was dismayed, but still hopeful. This was, after all, the Higher Culture that Miss Scanlon was always talking about, and perhaps it wasn't so easy to understand. I went downstairs and borrowed Nels's dictionary, but it didn't help much. Maybe I would understand them better some other time. Tomorrow. Yes, I promised myself, tomorrow I would read them thoroughly. Tomorrow, I would start copying off the precious secrets.

But one tomorrow after another marched

by, and I did not get back to the pamphlets. Other interesting things were going on. Most important, Carmelita and I had become Best Friends. I became acquainted with the Vanetti family and was utterly fascinated by them.

Rose, Carmelita's older sister, worked at the five-and-ten down on Mission Street, and was going steady with the assistant manager. He came to see her almost every night and brought her big boxes of candy, which she gave to us because candy made her face break out.

There were three Vanetti boys, named — every one of them — Joseph. And no one in the family seemed to think that an unusual thing. "Oh," they would shrug, "Mama, she likes the name Joseph."

I would stay at Carmelita's just as late as I dared, to be there when Mrs. Vanetti went out on her porch to scream, "Joseph! Joseph! Joseph! Come home to the dinner!" And to hear three assorted voices answer "Com-ing, Mama!"

Then Christine's class took up volley ball, and because Carmelita and I were volley-ball players from way back, we immediately appointed ourselves coaches and mentors and trained them mercilessly after school and at every recess.

In truth, I had completely forgotten about the "How to Become a Famous Author" course until I received a letter from New York.

"We remind you," they chided gently, "that your remittance of $7.00 has not been received. Inasmuch as you kept the course over the specified five-day trial period, the amount is now due and payable." Hoping to hear from me immediately, they were sincerely mine.

I finally learned what the phrase "plumbing the nethermost depths of despair" really meant. Oh, how *could* I have kept the pamphlets too long? A frantic consultation with the calendar assured me that I had. Exactly sixteen days too long.

Where was I to ever get *seven whole dollars*? I, whose father worked hard and long, whose mother was taking in boarders to help support us? Panic-stricken, I rushed to Carmeltia. What, I wailed, was I going to *do*?

"You might," she suggested, "get children to take care of after school."

Our usual pay was ten cents a child. Feverishly I added and subtracted. How could I take care of seventy children within the thirty-day limit the New York people had given me?

Carmelita shrugged. "Perhaps the nine day novena — it would help."

But I was not a Catholic, and we were uncertain as to whether nine day novenas would work out under those circumstances.

All the while Carmelita and I badgered neighbors to let us take care of their children, long, official letters kept coming addressed to me, each succeeding letter more sternly worded. And I became more and more frightened.

In one last ultimate gesture of despair, I packed the straw suitcase and hid it in my attic. I had decided that it would be far better for Mama to have one less daughter than one who would have to go to jail. And oh, I mourned, how hopeful Mama had been that Winford was going to make me into a little *lady*!

It was Carmelita who finally brought the first ray of hope into my darkness. She had found a newspaper that was offering a fifty-dollar first prize for the best essay on Americanism. And not only that, we read, but it also offered a second prize of twenty dollars and three prizes of ten dollars each.

"You see?" Carmelita comforted. "With the fine course, you are sure to win one of the prizes."

I sobbed with relief. *Of course*! Very probably I'd win the first prize. My goodness, I'd have forty-three dollars left over.

We read on. The contest closed in nine days.

While I had every confidence in my seven-dollar How-to-Be-a-Writer pamphlets, something about that nine days seemed to me to be a sign — a portent.

"Tell me again," I said to Carmelita, "about this novena business."

She explained carefully. One went to Mass

for nine days and said prayers for one's intentions.

That, I said, would work out fine. She could make the novena; I would write the essay.

"But," she reminded me, "it is very hard for me to awaken in the mornings. How will I be able to get to church before school?"

That too was easy. Since she would be doing it entirely for me, what kind of a friend would I be if I could not wake her in time?

The mornings were foggy and cold, but Carmelita never complained. Every dawn found me outside her window, tapping impatiently on the glass. Within five minutes she would be out, yawning and rubbing her eyes, but wearing her Sunday hat. I would escort her to the doors of the church, then run home to consult my pamphlets and work on my essay.

On the closing day of the contest, we skated all the way downtown to the *Examiner* Building to deposit the essay. We weren't going to trust any post office or mailbox. Besides, we had no money for stamps.

We discovered two neighbors who had the *Examiner* delivered to their doors, and we took turns sneaking their paper and following news of the judging of the contest.

Finally, those welcome words, "See tomorrow's *Examiner* for the list of the essay winners."

Carmelita and I were huddled on the neighbor's steps when the paper boy came by. We waited until he was out of sight, then ruthlessly tore open the neatly folded newspaper.

Carmelita's shaking finger traced down the page. First Prize Winner — Second Prize Winner — Third Prize Winner. My name wasn't there! Fourth — Fifth — We looked at each other with frightened eyes and started reading again. Ah — my name!

I had got forty-fifth Honorable Mention.

But no prize.

Carmelita blew her nose while I rubbed my eyes hard.

"I didn't study the course hard enough," I said.

"Oh, no," my friend protested, "it must have been my fault. One morning I fell asleep in church and four times I yawned."

I had finally reached the end of my rope. I said a long farewell to Carmelita and went into the house to find Mama. I coaxed her upstairs to my attic, seated her in the one comfortable chair, and told her everything.

"It means so much to you, Katrin, this writing?" Mama questioned me gently.

"Oh, Mama, yes!' I cried.

"The stories, Katrin, you like to make them up?"

I sobbed loudly. Some day, I assured her, I would write great books. "It is something within me, Mama. Right here!" I pounded my chest dramatically.

Mama picked up the little gray pamphlets. "It is all here, then, how to do these great things you plan?"

Right there, I assured her. All I had to do was study 'em.

"We will find the money," Mama said.

And when I threw myself into her arms in an agony of gratefulness, she patted my back soothingly.

The rest of the family, however, were not so understanding.

Nels gave me a disgusted look and Christine said right out loud that I was getting away with murder. But Mama had Papa send away the seven-dollar money order and she clipped out the Honorable Mention column in the *Examiner* to show my name to Aunt Jenny.

Each night, Mama asked me how I was getting along with my study of the writing course, and each night I gravely assured her that I was learning more and more.

Then it was report-card time. I had never in my life got anything lower than an A, so I didn't even bother to open the envelope. I just carried it home to Mama.

We were alone in the kitchen, and while she was looking at my card, I broke off a piece of freshly baked fladbröd. Mama made a funny little sound. I looked up. She was staring at my card.

"A red letter F," she said slowly. "That is bad?"

"Bad?" I said. "My goodness, Mama, that's the very worst mark you can get. That's *failure*. Who got an F?"

"You did," Mama said. "In composition."

I stared with horror at the incriminating mark. *Composition F?* That book report I'd failed to turn in —

Desperately, I tried to make excuses, but Mama wouldn't listen.

"Katrin," she said severely. "That writing course we pay the seven dollars for — you march right upstairs and get it."

I marched. In a hurry. Returning, I laid the pamphlets on the table.

"Now," Mama said sternly, "you will sit down and copy off every one of the lessons."

"All of them?" I wailed.

Mama nodded. "Every word."

"But, Mama, it will take me *forever*!"

"Then," Mama was firm, "then you had better get started."

So I did.

8 ‌❧ *Mama*
and the Occasion

There was excitement at school.

Winford, it was whispered, was to have an exceedingly distinguished visitor.

Miss Grimes, our principal, called a special assembly to confirm the news. "We are to be honored," she announced, "by a visit from Mrs. Reed Winford, that gr-eat lady." Miss Grimes rolled her words like our minister did when he preached Damnation.

"Mrs. Winford is," she continued, "the widow of that gr-eat and no-ble educator for whom our school is named. She will be with us on Chuesday week."

Mrs. Reed Winford, we learned, was famous as an educator in her own right, and had been Dean of Women these many years in an important Eastern university.

Now, since Mrs. Winford intended to spend her sabbatical year in the Far East, she would stop over in San Francisco just long enough to greet the upper-grade pupils and the teaching staff of the school that was a monument to her husband.

Genteel excitement ran high among the teachers, but our eighth grade was not particularly interested until Miss Grimes gave us complete charge of the refreshments for the reception.

Miss Scanlon twittered with delight and appointed Hester Prinn the chairman. Hester took elocution lessons and knew how to speak pieces. She never blushed or seemed ill at ease when she had to stand up in front of the class.

Now she said: "Let us all work together, girls, to make this a never-to-be-forgotten *Occasion*. Wouldn't it be nice if several of us brought some special little tidbit from home? Made this a real fancy tea?"

Miss Scanlon smiled and nodded. Hester nodded back graciously and held her hands together, very ladylike. "I," she said condescendingly, "shall be glad to bring our silver tea service and our sterling silver cake plate from home for the Occasion. And the tea."

The girls clapped politely. And for one awful moment I hated Hester Prinn more than anything else in the world. I envied her her assurance and aplomb; I had never in my life seen a silver tea service, much less owned one — and I hadn't the slightest idea what a "tidbit" was.

"Now won't someone else," Hester begged prettily, "also volunteer?"

"My mother makes lovely currant cake," Madeline said.

"Splendid."

"And *mine* makes fancy little cucumber sandwiches when *she* has a tea. I know she will let me bring some." Thyra Marin smiled primly at the rest of us.

"Fine!" Hester said heartily. "Someone else?"

"Cookies?" Mary Weston offered shyly.

"Are they — fancy cookies?"

"Oh, yes. Frosted, and all in different shapes."

"Then by all means, cookies."

Carmelita raised her hand. "I'll bring something, I don't know what. I'll have to ask my mother."

Now I loved Carmelita dearly, but it was unthinkable that she be allowed to get ahead of me.

"I, too, will bring something," I announced loudly. I had no idea what it would be, and to forestall questions, I added hastily, "a tidbit — a special tidbit."

"Thank you all so very much," Hester said. "I appoint the girls who are contributing to be the serving committee."

Before school was dismissed that afternoon, I sneaked a glance in the big dictionary on Miss Scanlon's desk. "Tidbit," it said, "a choice morsel of food."

I breathed a sigh of relief.

When I got home from school I found Aunt Jenny in the kitchen visiting with Mama. I told them about the distinguished visitor that was coming to Winford and bragged about being appointed to the serving committee.

"Mama," I asked, "what do you cook specially well? A — a choice morsel?"

"I just cook plain," Mama said.

Aunt Jenny snorted. "You are too modest," she said. "I just wish I had your knack with pastry, with lutefisk." She closed her eyes. "And your kjödboller," she said dreamily, "in the cream sauce. Why, they melt in a person's mouth."

Mama blushed at Aunt Jenny's praise. "Perhaps," she conceded, "perhaps I do make the good kjödboller — the meat balls."

"Oh, Mama," I begged, "would you make some for me to take to the reception for Mrs. Winford?"

Mama did not think that meat balls were quite the appropriate dish for an Occasion. "Why not a cake?" she suggested.

"One of the girls already offered to bring a cake."

"Cookies, then? I will make kringler."

"No. Mary Weston's bringing cookies. And Thyra's mother is going to make cucumber sandwiches."

Aunt Jenny was shocked. Cucumbers? Didn't people know that fresh cucumbers were poisonous? Sandwiches, to her way of thinking, were a waste of time. "Give them something to eat," she said heartily, "something they can smack their lips over."

Mama looked uncertain. Had we forgotten that kjödboller must be served hot?

But Aunt Jenny and I disposed of Mama's gentle arguments, one after the other. I was obsessed with the idea of showing the clique what a wonderful cook my mother was; of bringing some tidbit that would so outshine the other contributions that the Occasion would stand out in their memories forever. The girls could not *help* liking me — wanting to be my friends — if I made the Occasion a big success.

And Aunt Jenny was determined that the poor teachers, "thin as sticks every one of them," should, for once in their lives, taste real food.

Keeping the meat balls hot? Easy. One of Aunt Jenny's neighbors had a contraption called a chafing dish that was guaranteed to keep food hot. And if Katrin would promise to be very careful of it —

"Oh, I *will*, Aunt Jenny."

Aunt Jenny planned it all out very capably.

The meat balls must be prepared in the morning, and I could come home for lunch on the day of the reception and take them back to school with me. Aunt Jenny would instruct me how to light the alcohol lamp under the contraption, and there you were. What was wrong with that idea?

Mama had to admit that it sounded all right.

Since Carmelita hadn't told the girls what she was going to bring, I decided not to tell about my wonderful contribution either.

"Wait and see," I told Hester when she asked me. "And will you be surprised!"

Hester and Madeline and Thyra were almost nice to me during the days we waited for the Occasion. Once they let me play in their jacks game, and twice they walked clear across the school yard with me during recess.

I was quietly happy. After the reception, I dreamed, after the teachers and Mrs. Reed Winford had smacked their lips over Mama's delicious meat balls, the girls would notice me even more.

"I simply *must* have the recipe," I could hear Miss Grimes say.

And Mrs. Winford would ask to meet the girl whose mother cooked so wonderfully. "Quite the nicest tidbit," she would say, "of this whole reception."

And the girls would smile and nod at me. They might even clap. And I wouldn't blush a bit.

"Chuesday week" finally arrived, and I rushed home at lunch time to get the tidbit.

Mama was flushed, but happy. "Never," she told me, "have I had such good luck with the kjödboller. Just taste."

I tasted, and assured her that she had indeed outdone herself. Flaky, tender, swimming in the creamy sauce, the meat balls looked like a picture out of a magazine.

Carefully, we transferred them to the chafing dish. And with many warnings, Mama gave me the tiny bottle of alcohol and a block of matches. Mama had a great fear of things blowing up.

It started to rain when I got to the corner, but I was too excited to go back home for my raincoat and umbrella. Shielding the precious burden as best I could, I raced the two blocks to school.

When I got there, Miss Scanlon sent me down to the furnace room to dry my shoes. On the way, I tiptoed into the auditorium and deposited the chafing dish on the long, white-clothed table that held Hester's gleaming silver tea service. I wasn't even jealous; the chafing dish looked every bit as nice.

When I got to the furnace room, the janitress was sitting on an upturned soap box, talking to herself.

"Reception," she was muttering. *"Reception."*

She looked at me sternly. "Don't I always keep this school clean?"

I nodded timidly and moved closer to the furnace.

"Better," she declared, "than any other janitress ever did. Ask anyone. Ask the Board of Education. They'll tell you that Mrs. Kronever, she takes pride in her work."

"Ha!" she continued. "Ha. Reception!" She rocked back and forth and glared at me. "Who," she demanded, "who works hardest at this Winford school? Tell me that."

"I guess you do, Mrs. Kronever."

She made her eyes small. "Then why am I not asked to the Reception too?"

"I — I don't know."

"Ha!" she said again. "All right, all right. Let them have their old Reception. Without me!"

I stood up. Wet shoes or not I'd better get back to the classroom. This, I decided, was what Miss Scanlon meant when she said that Mrs. Kronever was temperamental. I made my escape, leaving the janitress to her dark mutterings.

The afternoon session dragged by. A cold

and driving rain had darkened the day, and we shivered. Three times Miss Scanlon had to send girls down to Mrs. Kronever with requests for more heat, without tangible results.

Dismissal bell finally rang, and the lower grades were sent home. We favored ones in the eighth congregated in the hall outside the auditorium, waiting with the teachers for Miss Grimes and the Distinguished Visitor.

For the first time, I noticed that Carmelita held a long paper-wrapped package.

"What did you bring?" I whispered, hoping anxiously that it would not be something to compete with the delectable meat balls.

"A bottle of fine wine," she whispered back, and tore off a piece of the paper to show me the bottle, cased in straw.

I shuddered. A faint doubt entered my mind. Were we doing the right thing, Carmelita and I? Of course, meat balls were different from *wine* — but —

"What will Miss Grimes say?" I asked anxiously.

Camelita shrugged. "The wine," she said, "is very good for the stommack."

I remembered the lecture Miss Grimes had given us on the evils of rum. Had she mentioned wine? I was torn between two loyalties; I did not want to hurt my friend's feelings, nor did I want her held up to the ridicule of the school.

"Wrap it up again," I implored her. "Let me think."

"Is good for the stommack," Carmelita persisted, and tore off the rest of the wrapping.

Miss Grimes came bustling down the hall then, followed by a tall gray-haired lady in a fitted black suit. We stood back bashfully and Miss Grimes opened the auditorium door with a flourish and bade our Distinguished Visitor enter.

We trooped after her, I to my chosen place by the chafing dish, along with the other members of the serving committee; the rest of the class and the teachers to chairs placed in front of the platform.

The pungent odor of meat balls greeted us, and I sniffed appreciatively as I lighted the lamp under the chafing dish. Miss Grimes looked uncomfortable and wrinkled her nose a little, but she gave a wonderful introduction to the Distinguished Visitor.

Mrs. Winford was a beautiful lady. She stood up and told us how happy she was to be with us; how she had looked forward to meeting us all — I lost the rest of the speech because Hester was motioning to Miss Scanlon from the doorway, and I was curious.

I began to notice how cold it was in the auditorium and wondered why someone didn't turn on the lights. Then Miss Scanlon rushed in and whispered something to Miss Grimes and Miss Grimes rushed out the door.

Mrs. Winford finished talking and we clapped politely. She stood there on the platform until Miss Grimes came rushing back again. Miss Grimes's face had turned awful red.

"*Most* unfortunate," she announced, "but we are unable to find our janitress. She — she forgot to turn on the heat. And, stupidly enough, she has also gone off with the key to the domestic science room and the girls cannot get in to use the stove to boil the water for tea.

"But if you will just be patient," she promised, "we will have everything under way very shortly. I know we are all anxious for our tea."

Mrs. Winford looked as if she could do with a cup of hot tea. But she just smiled graciously and held her coat more tightly around herself. Miss Scanlon sneezed, twice, and Miss Grimes glared at her. The teachers went on vain expeditions for the missing janitress.

Miss Grimes and the teachers sat in a group by the platform and made valiant conversation with our shivering guest, while the nerves of the serving committee became increasingly edgy. We watched the dainty little cucumber sandwiches become soggy and limp. Madeline tried to cut the currant cake with the cake server, and it fell into crumbs. Hester made futile little dashes from the tea table to the hall.

"It's getting late," Hester fretted, "and colder. Miss Lyons thinks she may have a key to the domestic science room at her home. She's gone to see. If we stand around much longer, we'll freeze." She noticed Carmelita. "What in the world," Hester asked crossly, "are you holding?"

"Wine."

"Wine? *Wine*? Don't you know that all teachers are W.C.T.U.?"

I didn't know what W.C.T.U. was, but Carmelita was my best friend. "It is good," I parroted, "for the stommack."

"They'll probably *expel* you!" Hester hissed.

Carmelita gulped, but held tightly to the wine.

"And what are *you* being so mysterious about?" Hester asked me impatiently. "What have you got in that old chafing dish?"

Reverently, I lifted the cover. "Meat balls," I breathed. "In cream sauce."

It was the signal for laughter. Harsh and high-pitched laughter, vainly smothered by crammed handkerchiefs. Hester and Madeline and Thyra giggled and sputtered; then held tightly to one another and kept repeating "Meat balls!" "To a fancy tea she brings *meat balls*!"

From her seat by the platform, Miss Grimes

frowned at the unseemly noise and signaled us to be quiet.

The girls wiped streaming eyes— looked at me — and collapsed into one another's arms again.

"Meat balls!" Hester grimaced. "*Poor* people eat meat balls."

"For *dinner,* if ever," Madeline hiccuped, "not at a tea."

My cheeks burned. My eyes smarted. But I dared not let the tears fall. Nobody liked my lovely, lovely surprise. Soon now Miss Grimes and Mrs. Winford would discover my stupidity. And the teachers. And everyone would laugh and laugh. And never, now, would my classmates be friendly.

Through the haze of unshed tears I saw my sister Christine.

She was standing by the tea table, holding out my raincoat and rubbers. "Mama sent me back with them," she said matter-of-factly. "It's pouring out."

"Go home!" I whispered fiercely, "Go home!"

Her calm gaze went to the table — to the girls. "I heard — " she began.

"Go home!" I clutched her arm, pulled her out of earshot of the still giggling girls. "If you dare tell Mama — "

Christine shook off my hand. "You and Carmelita should have known better," she said reasonably. "Mama should have known better."

"But her feelings will be hurt, Christine," I pleaded. "Please don't ever tell." Quickly I explained about the janitress. Christine shrugged, and with a cool look at the girls standing by the table, she moved away.

And I watched her go — envying her from the bottom of my aching heart. Christine *would* have known better. Christine had been born knowing the proper things. She was never impulsive, headstrong. Never did foolish, stupid things. Christine moved calmly and clearly through life, serene and — invulnerable.

Miss Grimes mounted the platform to announce that since it was getting late, and stormier, all but the girls on the serving committee would be dismissed.

Those of us left stood awkwardly about the tea table. Madeline and Hester would look at the chafing dish and then make silly faces at each other. I examined the tips of my shoes with infinite care. Carmelita moved closer to me, as if for comfort.

It got darker and colder.

One by one, the teachers made their excuses and escaped.

At last, only the serving committee, the Distinguished Visitor, and Miss Grimes were left.

"Miss Lyons should certainly be here with

the key soon," Miss Grimes fretted. "Hark! I hear someone coming along the hall."

We watched the doorway hopefully.

And Mama came in!

In her arms she carried two bulky newspaper-wrapped packages.

I rushed over to her, words tumbling from my lips.

"Christine already brought my rain things, Mama."

Silently, desperately, I prayed: Please, oh, please, let Mama go back home before she finds out. If Christine had told! If the girls dared to laugh at my mother —

Mama smiled at me and walked right over to Miss Grimes and Mrs. Winford.

"You will catch cold," she scolded gently. "You need the good hot coffee to warm you up."

Mrs. Winford laughed ruefully. "What wouldn't I give," she sighed, "for a cup of hot coffee!"

Miss Grimes sneezed violently.

Mama clucked sympathetically. "See now what I have brought. Wrapped in the newspaper to keep the warmth." She herded us down to the tea table, smiled at Hester, Thyra, Mary, Madeline, and Carmelita.

She set her packages down. "In this one — the hot coffee." Mama brought forth our copper pitcher, fragrant steam escaping from it.

"And in this one," she unwrapped the other package, "is the hot chocolate for Katrin's friends."

Within a few minutes, Mama had us all comfortably seated about the tea table. Mrs. Winford and Miss Grimes drank great loud draughts of the steaming coffee. The girls and I were just as greedy with the blessedly hot chocolate.

Mama was always good at making folks comfortable. Now she passed the fancy cookies and the crumbs of currant cake. She said that Mary's cookies were about the nicest she had ever tasted, and she complimented Madeline on the delicious cake. She also commiserated with Thyra about the collapse of the cucumber sandwiches, and wholeheartedly admired Hester's tea set.

Warm and relaxed, we finally drained the last drop of coffee and of chocolate. Miss Grimes thanked Mama so sincerely that she seemed like a different person from the austere principal we were so used to. She thanked the serving committee too, and said that she was proud of us. She said that although we had been confronted with a trying situation, the cold — and the long wait — we had acted like Little Ladies throughout.

Mrs. Winford complimented us too. And when she was leaving, she took Mama's hands in both of hers, and they spoke together for a long time.

After Miss Grimes and the visitor had gone, we began to clear the table. Mama worked with us. Hester started to speak several times. Finally she blurted: "I would — excuse me, but — I would like to taste the — meat balls."

I gulped indignantly and started to say something, but Mama shook her head at me. Serenely, she took a clean saucer, heaped it with kjödboller, and passed it to Hester. Hester tasted bravely. "Why," she said wonderingly, "why, they're delicious."

And as the rest of us passed our saucers to Mama for portions, she spoke of other Norwegian dishes. Of svisker gröd, of the festive Yule kage, and pannkaka med lingon. The girls seemed interested.

"You must bring your friends to our home, Katrin," Mama said to me. "I will make for you the Norske kroner — the Norwegian cookies."

I didn't, couldn't, answer.

"Perhaps," Mama continued quietly, "the girls would like to see the baby Kaaren."

Hester's face got pink. "A baby? Have you a baby at your house?"

Mama nodded and smiled.

"We had a baby once," Hester said softly. "My little brother. We — we lost him."

"Kathryn has a big attic too!" Carmelita bragged loudly.

"An attic all your very own?" Madeline asked.

I looked at the girls. Their faces were friendly.

"Next Wednesday," Mama said. "Come next Wednesday after school. We will make of it a party, yes?"

The girls said they would come. We locked the auditorium door and went out into the school yard. Hester, Madeline, Thyra, and Mary not only smiled as they left but waved too, and said, "Last look!"

Carmelita and I trudged after Mama.

"The wine," I remembered suddenly. "What of the wine?"

"Under the table your Mama put it," Carmelita said succinctly. "For Mrs. Kronever, maybe."

"It will be good," I joked, "for her stommack."

And Carmelita and I giggled happily all the way home.

9 ✑ Mama
and the Doctor's Wife

Papa was not well. He never complained, but we began to notice how heavily he sat in his chair these evenings, how often he put a hand to his head.

When he saw us looking at him, he would make little jokes about his laziness, pretend it was the laziness that kept him from finishing the work on the porch — from putting up the shelves in Miss Durant's room.

Then Mama's face would whiten and she would question Papa anxiously in Norwegian.

"Is nothing, lille ven." He would try to smile. "It will pass."

And when Mama would put her cool hands against his head, Papa would close his eyes and sigh. "That is good," he would say, "that makes the pounding stop."

But as the days passed, even Mama's gentle rubbing did not serve to stop the pounding. She would hold her hands under the running water to make them cold, then put them against Papa's head, but the torture in his eyes would not lessen.

Then one afternoon he came home early from work.

We were all in the kitchen, and when Papa stumbled in, it was as if the end of the world had come. Only during strikes or lockouts did men come home in the daytime.

Papa pretended that his head hurt just a little, but when he was not able to drink the coffee that Mama made for him, she said he must be really ill. And without giving Papa time to protest, she sent Nels for Dr. Johnson in a hurry, and had Christine and me put clean sheets on the bed.

But before we could help Papa into the bedroom, he gave a funny little sound and toppled right out of his chair onto the floor. He lay there all crumpled up and his hoarse breathing sounded loud and terrible in the silence.

Dagmar and I began to cry, but for once Mama didn't pay any attention to us. She dropped to her knees and cradled Papa's head in her arms, speaking to him softly, wiping the froth off his lips with her clean handkerchief.

Even when Dr. Johnson and Nels came hurrying in, Mama didn't move. The doctor examined Papa right on the floor. He asked quick, sharp questions. Had Papa ever had a head injury? Had he fallen lately?

Mama said no, he had never fallen before, but two years ago, on the City Hall job, a scantling had struck him.

Dr. Johnson nodded and stood up. "That may be it," he said. "It acts like a brain injury of some kind. Of course, cannot tell definitely until we take X rays. However, immediate hospitalization is indicated. I'll send an ambulance."

Mama straightened up then, but she kept a trembling hand against Papa's cheek.

"If I can be with him," she said. "Whatever hospital he goes to, they must allow me to stay with him."

Dr. Johnson flushed. I guess he was thinking of the time the clinic hospital tried to keep Mama from seeing Dagmar.

"St. Joseph's is not too expensive," he said gruffly, "and the nuns are fine nurses."

Mama said, "Will they let me stay with him?"

"He will have the best of care," Dr. Johnson said.

Mama said, "Will they let me stay with him?"

Dr. Johnson harrumphed and said that he would arrange it so.

He left then, and Mama had Nels take all

the money out of the Little Bank and put it into her purse. There wasn't very much. She had Christine write down all the things to do for the baby; the groceries that would be needed from the store; and what to give Miss Durant for her dinner.

Her voice was as calm and quiet as always, but to me it seemed as if Mama had gone far away and left a white-faced stranger kneeling in her place.

Only when the men from the ambulance came in did Mama stand up and put on her coat and her hat. She made the men be very careful about lifting Papa, she tucked an extra blanket over the stretcher, then kissed us all good-bye.

After Mama left, we children and Nels just sat on in the kitchen. We looked at the list Christine had made; we knew we should be fixing dinner — but it seemed as if we couldn't get started.

When Nels put on his coat to go down to the grocery store, Dagmar began to cry again.

"I'll take her with me then," Nels said.

Christine and I looked at each other. Suddenly, it became terribly important for all of us to stay together. Christine and I ran for our coats too, wrapped Baby Kaaren in her warmest blanket, and trudged to the store after Nels and Dagmar.

And when we got back, we just sat around some more.

I guess it was a good thing that Aunt Jenny happened to stop in on her way home from downtown. She put us all to work in a hurry, and for once we welcomed her bossiness. She fixed Miss Durant's dinner, fed Kaaren and put her down to sleep, and cooked enough food for several days. Then she went down to the drugstore to telephone.

In a little while, the other Aunts started coming in. Aunt Trina was first. She sat very close to her new husband, Mr. Thirkelsen, and cried a little every time Papa's name was mentioned.

Aunt Marta and Uncle Ole brought us a big bag of red apples. We thanked them politely and put the apples in the glass dish in the center of the table. Nobody ate any though.

When Aunt Sigrid and Uncle Peter came in, Aunt Jenny put the coffeepot on and told Christine to set out the cups and saucers.

Uncle Peter still wore his plasterer's overalls, and his hands and face were white from plaster dust. Aunt Sigrid apologized for his appearance.

"We did not want to wait until he cleaned up," she explained. "When we heard — when Jenny telephoned — we were so anxious — " She looked at us children and stopped talking.

But it was too late. Dagmar and I began to cry again. Aunt Trina coaxed Dagmar to sit on her lap and Mr. Thirkelsen gave us each a nickel.

Then Mama came in.

Everyone jumped to help her take off her coat, to give her a chair, to pour her coffee. We all asked questions at once, and Aunt Jenny scolded us loudly.

"Cannot you let her get her breath?" she demanded. "Cannot you let her drink the hot coffee?"

Then Aunt Jenny did a very curious thing. She went into the bedroom and brought out a sleepy-eyed Kaaren and put her in Mama's arms.

"Of all things!" Aunt Trina protested. "To waken a baby out of a sound sleep!"

Aunt Jenny glared at her. "She is warmly wrapped, is she not? Will the world end, then, if a baby misses a small hour of sleep?"

Easy to see, she added gruffly, that Trina had never been a mother.

I looked at Mama. She held Kaaren very close and smoothed the soft down on her tiny head, folded the blanket around the small pink feet. I guess maybe holding the baby did comfort Mama, because the white line around her mouth went away, and a little color came into her cheeks.

Then Mama spoke. "He — Papa has not awakened yet."

"Still unconscious?"

Mama nodded. "They took — pictures. Nels?"

"X rays, Mama."

"That is right. X rays. Dr. Johnson says there is something pressing against the brain. Something caused, perhaps by an old injury." She looked at Uncle Ole and Uncle Peter. "You remember the City Hall job? You worked on it with him."

The Uncles both nodded. "A scantling fell on him," Uncle Ole said. "But he seemed all right at the time. As I remember, he worked through to the end of the shift."

"Yes. But the hurt — the blow started something. It is hard to understand. The doctor tried to explain — but they — " Mama took a deep breath — "they say that they must operate as soon as is possible."

Aunt Jenny got up and poured more coffee. "That Dr. Johnson," she said, "is a very fine doctor."

Aunt Sigrid patted Mama's shoulder. "Jenny is right. Surely there is no need for worry when you have Dr. Johnson."

Mama looked down at the tablecloth. "But Dr. Johnson," she whispered, "says it is too serious an operation. He says it will take someone with greater skill — greater learning. A — a specialist."

"Well, then," Aunt Jenny said firmly, "we shall have the specialist. Excuse me a moment." She went into the bedroom. When she came out, she was fastening the front of her dress and carrying a small chamois bag. She laid the bag on the table in front of Mama.

"There are five twenty-dollar gold pieces there," she said. "I have no need of them."

Mr. Thirkelsen looked at Aunt Trina. When she nodded he jumped to his feet and pulled a long black leather purse out of his pocket and emptied it on the table.

"Thirty-six dollars and forty-three cents," he said.

Mr. Thirkelsen was a bookkeeper and very exact.

Aunt Trina beamed at the Aunts.

"We have this fifty dollars put by," Aunt Sigrid said. "Of what good is it lying around?"

"Here is thirty-five more," Uncle Ole said. "No — please do not say anything. Tomorrow is my pay night."

I had never seen Mama cry, but when she lifted her head that night and looked at the Aunts and the Uncles, her eyes were misty.

She tried to thank them, but they all protested and talked very loudly. Mama's lips trembled and Uncle Ole interrupted brusquely: "I will come by on Sunday to finish closing in the back porch and putting up the shelves."

Uncle Ole was a fine carpenter.

Uncle Peter asked wistfully if there wasn't some plastering Mama wanted done.

Mama smiled a little, but shook her head.

Then the Aunts kissed Mama good-bye, and the Uncles shook hands all around.

"What is the specialist doctor's name?" Aunt Jenny wanted to know.

"Dr. Beauchamp. Dr. Johnson says he is the best in the city. I shall see him first thing tomorrow and arrange everything."

Mama took me with her to the hospital the next morning, but we found that it was not so easy to see the great specialist doctor.

Dr. Johnson was waiting for us at the desk.

"Papa?" Mama asked quickly. "He still — sleeps?"

Dr. Johnson nodded. "Probably won't regain consciousness until after the operation."

"Then," Mama said, "we must not wait. We shall have the Dr. Beauchamp and — "

"Very unusual!" Dr. Johnson interrupted suddenly. "Very unusual procedure! Never heard of such a thing."

I jumped.

"This Beauchamp," Dr. Johnson explained. "Splendid doctor, splendid. Fine surgeon. Foreign. Doesn't speak much English. Got a wife.

89

Calls herself Madame Beauchamp. *She* informs me that all operative arrangements must be made with her."

He looked at Mama sharply. "I tried to talk with the woman. Quarreled. She's a devil. Says you must make all arrangements with her. Financial or — or financial."

Mama smiled relievedly. "That is all right, then. We have money."

Dr. Johnson harrumphed and looked down at his shoes.

"Now you are not to worry about me," he barked, "or the hospital — take care of that later. But this Beauchamp business — this Madame person — here" — he scribbled an address on a card — "you must go and talk to her. Try to — Beauchamp, you understand, is the man for the job — must have him. Oh, hell! Maybe the woman's got a heart. Here!" He thrust the card into Mama's hand and walked down the hall, muttering angrily to himself.

Mama and I took the streetcar out to the Parnassus Hill district. Dr. Beauchamp's house turned out to be an old brownstone mansion, set far back in a neglected garden.

A very tall lady with black, black hair answered Mama's timid knock. "Come in, come in," she said briskly. When Mama started to tell her who we were, she broke in with "Yes,

yes, I know. Spoke to Johnson already. Very rude person. Exceedingly rude person."

She herded us into a long gloomy room that was full of spindly legged furniture. We sat down gingerly and Madame Beauchamp bustled about, opening doors, putting up window shades, talking all the while.

"We've just moved in," she shouted at us. "Can't get any workmen to fix this place up. Robbers, all of them. Ask outlandish prices. These old homes. So dark, so gloomy. The doctor and I — we must have scope. Vista."

"The doctor," Mama said, "please — may we see the doctor?"

"Ah," said Madame Beauchamp, "that is the trouble. Everyone wants to see the doctor."

She sat down by Mama.

"That's exactly the reason," she said confidingly, "why I have had to take over the — the mundane part of Doctor's business."

Mama looked at her helplessly.

Madame Beauchamp settled back in her chair. "Dr. Beauchamp is a genius," she said. "There is magic — sheer magic — in his hands." She held out her own large capable hands and looked at them for a moment.

"But not in his head," she conceded at last. "About money matters, Doctor is as a child." She smiled at Mama brightly. "Would you believe it," she asked, "that before I took over, the dear man was doing intricate unbelievable operations for practically *nothing*? Let someone but come to him with a sad story — let them but — "

"My husband," Mama said simply, "is very ill. He needs the operation immediately. We have come to make the arrangements."

Madame Beauchamp rushed over to a pale green and gold desk and all but knocked it over getting a receipt book and a pencil.

"Ah, yes," she said. "Dr. Johnson told me. Now let us see — " She looked at Mama out of the corners of her eyes. "You understand, of course, that an operation of that type is quite — well, shall we say — "

"How much will be be?" Mama asked.

"A doctor's training is long and expensive," Madame Beauchamp said. "Even doctors have obligations — expenses to meet." She gazed around at the dark walls and shuddered. "Will you just look how that wall cramps this room?" She pointed dramatically. "It must be torn out. We must have scope! Vista! One large, airy, beautiful room — "

"How much," Mama asked wearily, "how much for the operation?"

Madame Beauchamp closed her mouth with a snap.

"Three hundred and fifty dollars!"

I sat back in my chair with a thump. Mama gasped.

"But — but Madame Beauchamp — I have just the two hundred and twenty-five dollars."

"Splendid," boomed Madame Beauchamp. "You only need a hundred and twenty-five more."

"But that — that is impossible."

"Well, I'll tell you what I'll do. I'll reduce the price to three hundred dollars even."

Mama only shook her head helplessly.

"Ah, but surely you have relatives? Friends? Couldn't you — borrow?"

"My sisters — their husbands — they have already given of their utmost."

"Ah, well, that is your little problem. The operation will be three hundred dollars. Not a penny less."

Mama clasped her hands tightly. "Papa, he must have the operation today. So I will give you the two hundred and twenty-five dollars now and we will pay the rest as soon as — "

"No," Madame Beauchamp interrupted. "It must be in cash."

Mama looked stricken.

The doctor's wife stood up. "Do you know," she said, "I find that when people *have* to get money — they generally do. Somehow. Good day."

Mama stumbled a little going out the gate. "Katrin," she said, "Oh, Katrin!"

"I think," I gulped, "I think I'm going to cry again."

Mama held tight to my arm. "Wait," she said, "wait. I just think of something."

She turned and ran up the path again and pounded on the door.

Madame Beauchamp opened it and smiled tightly at us.

"Ah," she said, "back so soon? How quickly you found the needed seventy-five dollars."

Mama didn't answer. She walked right back into the front room and stood by the green and gold desk. She opened her purse and counted out all the money that was there and laid it on the desk. Then she turned to the doctor's wife.

"There," she said firmly, "is every penny that we have in the world. But for the rest, I will get a man for you to do all your alteration work. And do it well."

"Ah," said Madame Beauchamp, eyeing the pile of silver and currency, paying particular attention to Aunt Jenny's gold pieces. "Ah, a new idea in barter, eh? I see. And this man — I will not have to pay him for his labor? It will apply on your — er — account?"

Mama nodded and watched Madame's hands stray toward the money.

"Very well," the doctor's wife decided suddenly. "Very well, it is a bargain. Here is your receipt and I will have Doctor at St. Joseph's Hospital within an hour."

As soon as we got back to the hospital and told them that Dr. Beauchamp was on his way, the nuns put Papa on a long table, covered him with a blanket, and wheeled him down the hall. They let me kiss his cheek, but he did not open his eyes.

All the while we waited outside the operating room for the specialist doctor to arrive, Mama held tightly to one of Papa's hands.

"In a little while," she kept saying — just as if he could hear her — "in a little while now, all will be well."

A door banged down the long hall, and a short, mustached little man came striding along, Madame Beauchamp following him.

"That is Dr. Beauchamp," the youngest nun whispered to Mama.

Madame Beauchamp came up to us and introduced her husband.

The great doctor bowed gallantly and put a quick hand on Papa's wrist. "We shall operate at once," he said. "I have but to change."

"Wait," Mama said. "Please — " Her eyes searched the doctor's kind face. "Forgive me — but you will be very careful?"

"Such impudence!" the doctor's wife said.

But the doctor smiled sympathetically. "Of

a certainty," he said to Mama. "Do not have the worry."

"Ah, yes, and one other thing," the doctor's wife broke in. "When will you be sending the man you spoke of? The one that is to do the alterations for me?"

Mama took a deep breath. "Just as soon as he is able, Madame Beauchamp."

"What?"

Mama put her hand on Papa's shoulder. *"This* is the man."

The doctor's wife shrieked.

"My goodness!" she cried. "But he may not — what if — oh, this is terrible! Doctor! You must be *very* careful!"

The doctor looked at his wife, then he looked at Mama. And his eyes began to twinkle. He came over and took both Mama's hands in his.

"Madame," he said, "I salute you. And I promise you that your husband — he will be all right."

Mama sighed happily. "That is good," she said. "That is good."

10 § Mama
and the Graduation Present

During the last week that Papa was in the hospital, we rented the big downstairs bedroom to two brothers, Mr. Sam and Mr. George Stanton.

The Stantons worked in the office of the Gas and Electric Company, and they paid a whole month's rent in advance, which was a very good thing for us. They were nice young men, and after dinner every night they would come out to the kitchen to tell Mama how much they enjoyed her cooking.

After they got better acquainted with Miss Durant, they teased her about her "rabbit food" and made bets with each other as to which one of them would be the first to coax her to eat a big thick steak — medium rare.

Mama was very proud of her three boarders; she listened to their chattering and laughter and said it was going to be fine when we had the hospital bills paid up and the money back to the Aunts. Then we would get more furniture and more boarders. Enough to fill all the chairs in the dining room. The Stanton brothers said they knew two more men from their place who would like to board with us.

On the day that Papa came home from the hospital, it was like a big party. We all stayed home from school and Mama let Dagmar decorate the table real fancy.

Everything seemed all right again when Papa walked carefully into the kitchen and sat down in the rocking chair. His face was white, and he looked thinner, but his smile was just the same. He had a bandage on his head and he made little jokes about how they shaved off his hair when he wasn't looking.

It was strange, having Papa about the house during the day, but it was nice too. He would be there in the kitchen when I came home from school and I would tell him all that had happened.

Winford School had become the most important thing in life to me. I was finally friends with the girls, and Carmelita and I were invited to all their parties. Every other Wednesday they came to my house and we would sit up in my attic, drink chocolate, eat cookies, and make plans about our graduation.

We discussed "High" and vowed that we would stay together all through the next four years. We were the only ones in our class going on to Lowell. Lowell, we told each other loftily, was "academic."

We were enthralled with our superiority. *We* were going to be the first class at Winford to have evening graduation exercises; *we* were having a graduation play; *we* were making our own graduation dresses in sewing class.

And when I was given the second lead in the play — the part of the Grecian boy — I found my own great importance hard to bear. I alone of all the girls had to go downtown to the costumer's to rent a wig. A coarse black wig that smelled of disinfectant, but made me feel like Geraldine Farrar. At every opportunity I would put it on and have Papa listen to my part of the play.

Then the girls started talking about graduation presents.

Madeline said she was getting an onyx ring with a small diamond. Hester was getting a real honest-to-goodness wristwatch, and Thyra's family was going to add seven pearls to the necklace they had started for her when she was a baby. Even Carmelita was getting something special: her sister Rose was putting a dollar every payday onto an ivory manicure set.

I was intrigued, and wondered what great surprise my family had in store for me. I talked about it endlessly, hoping for some clue. It would be terrible if my present were not as nice as the rest.

"It is the custom, then," Mama asked, "the giving of gifts when one graduates?"

"My goodness, Mama," I said, "it's practically the most important time in a girl's life — when she graduates."

I had seen a beautiful pink celluloid dresser set at Mr. Schiller's drugstore, and I set my heart upon it. I dropped hint after hint, until Nels took me aside and reminded me that we did not have money for that sort of thing. Had I forgotten that the Aunts and the hospital must be paid up? That just as soon as Papa was well enough he must do the Beauchamp job for no pay?

"I don't care," I cried recklessly, "I *must* have a graduation present. Why, Nels, think how I will feel if I don't get any. When the girls ask me — "

Nels got impatient and said he thought I was turning into a spoiled brat. And I retorted that since he was a boy he naturally couldn't be expected to understand certain things.

When Mama and I were alone one day she asked me how I would like her silver brooch for a graduation present. Mama thought a lot of that brooch — it had been her mother's.

"Mama," I said reasonably, "what in the world would I want an old brooch for?"

"It would be like a — an heirloom, Katrin. It was your grandmother's."

"No thank you, Mama."

"I could polish it up, Katrin."

I shook my head. "Look, Mama, a graduation present is something like — well, like that beautiful dresser set in Mr. Schiller's window."

There now, I had told. Surely, with such a hint —

Mama looked worried, but she didn't say anything. Just pinned the silver brooch back on her dress.

I was so sure that Mama would find some way to get me the dresser set, I bragged to the girls as if it were a sure thing. I even took them by Schiller's window to admire it. They agreed with me that it was wonderful. There was a comb, a brush, a mirror, a pincushion, a clothes brush. and even something called a hair-receiver.

Graduation night was a flurry of excitement.

I didn't forget a single word of my part in the play. Flushed and triumphant, I heard Miss Scanlon say that I was every bit as good as Hester, who had taken elocution lessons for years. And when I went up to the platform for my diploma, the applause for me was long and loud. Of course the Aunts and Uncles were all there, and Uncle Ole and Uncle Peter could clap very loud, but I pretended that it was because I was so popular.

And when I got home — there was the pink celluloid dresser set!

Mama and Papa beamed at my delight, but Nels and Christine, I noticed, didn't say anything. I decided that they were jealous, and felt sorry that they would not join me in my joy.

I carried the box up to my attic and placed the comb and brush carefully on my dresser. It took me a long while to arrange everything to my satisfaction. The mirror, so. The pincushion, here. The hair-receiver, there.

Mama let me sleep late the next morning. When I got down for breakfast, she had already gone downtown to do her shopping. Nels was reading the want-ad section of the paper. Since it was vacation he was going to try to get a job. He read the jobs aloud to Papa and they discussed each one.

After my breakfast, Christine and I went upstairs to make the beds. I made her wait while I ran up to my attic to look again at my wonderful present. Dagmar came with me, and when she touched the mirror, I scolded her so hard she started to cry.

Christine came up then and wiped Dagmar's tears and sent her down to Papa. She looked at me for a long time.

"Why do you look at me like that, Christine?"

"What do you care? You got what you wanted, didn't you?" She pointed to the dresser set. "Trash," she said, "cheap trash."

"Don't you *dare* talk about my lovely present like that! You're jealous, that's what. I'll tell Mama on you."

"And while you're telling her," Christine said, "ask her what she did with her silver brooch. The one her very own mother gave her. Ask her that."

I looked at Christine with horror. "What?" You mean — Did Mama — ?"

Christine walked away.

I grabbed up the dresser set and ran down the stairs to the kitchen. Papa was drinking his second cup of coffee, and Dagmar was playing with her doll in front of the stove. Nels had left.

"Papa, oh, Papa!" I cried. "Did Mama — Christine says — " I started to cry then, and Papa had me sit on his lap.

"There now," he said, and patted my shoulder. "There now."

And he dipped a cube of sugar into his coffee and fed it to me. We were not allowed to drink coffee — even with lots of milk in it — until we were considered grown up, but all of us children loved that occasional lump of sugar dipped in coffee.

After my hiccuping and sobbing had stopped, Papa talked to me very seriously. It was like this, he said. I had wanted the graduation present. Mama had wanted my happiness more than she had wanted the silver brooch. So she had traded it to Mr. Schiller for the dresser set.

"But I never wanted her to do that, Papa. If I had known — I would never have let her — "

"It was what Mama wanted to do, Katrin."

"But she *loved* it so. It was all she had of Grandmother's."

"She always meant it for you, Katrin."

I stood up slowly. I knew what I must do.

And all the way up to Mr. Schiller's drugstore, the graduation present in my arms, I thought of how hard it must have been for Mama to ask Mr. Schiller to take the brooch as payment. It was never easy for Mama to talk to strangers.

Mr. Schiller examined the dresser set with care. He didn't know, he said, about taking it back. After all, a bargain was a bargain, and he had been thinking of giving the brooch to his wife for her birthday next month.

Recklessly, I mortgaged my vacation.

If he would take back the dresser set, if he would give me back the brooch, I would come in and work for him every single day, even Saturdays.

"I'll shine the showcases," I begged. "I'll sweep the floor for you."

Mr. Schiller said that would not be necessary. Since I wanted the brooch back so badly, he would call the deal off. But if I was serious about working during vacation, he might be able to use me.

So I walked out of Mr. Schiller's drugstore not only with Mama's brooch, but with a job that started the next morning. I felt very proud. The dresser set suddenly seemed a childish and silly thing.

I put the brooch on the table in front of Papa.

He looked at me proudly. "Was it so hard to do, Daughter?"

"Not so hard as I thought." I pinned the brooch on my dress. "I'll wear it always," I said. "I'll keep it forever."

"Mama will be glad, Katrin."

Papa dipped a lump of sugar and held it out to me. I shook my head. "Somehow," I said, "I just don't feel like it, Papa."

"So?" Papa said. "So?"

And he stood up and poured out a cup of coffee and handed it to me.

"For me?" I asked wonderingly.

Papa smiled and nodded. "For my grown-up daughter," he said.

I sat up straight in my chair. And felt very proud as I drank my first cup of coffee.

11 &⬦ *Mama*
and Big Business

The family suffered (the younger members not in silence) during the weeks that followed my graduation. The weeks that I was in the employ of Schiller & Son, Druggists. A. Schiller, Prop.

Overnight I became an authority on all medical matters. At home, Latin phrases rolled glibly from my tongue. I never said "distilled water." No. It was "aqua distillati" the way it was printed on the square bottles in the drugstore. Nels knew some Latin, but I caught him on aqua menthapep and aqua auranti flora.

"My goodness," I crowed, "imagine not knowing that they mean peppermint and orange-flower water."

I ignored Nels's disgusted snort, and bragged endlessly concerning my importance, my indispensability to Mr. Schiller. Nor was I above wondering, often and audibly, how he had *ever* got along without me.

I think that if it had been left to Mrs. Schiller, she would have continued getting along without me. She had disapproved of Mr. Schiller's hiring me in the first place. Even when Mr. Schiller pointed out that it would mean that she wouldn't have to give up her afternoons to working in the store and having *that* to complain of, she just got crosser. It was Mrs. Schiller who decreed that I must work one month before getting my salary.

I worked at the drugstore for three hours every afternoon and all of Saturday morning. At first I simply shined the showcases and dusted the displays, lingering long and rapturously over the candy counter.

Then I was allowed to fill capsules. Quinine. In two-, three-, and five-grain doses. Even the fact that the quinine had a way of lingering on my hands for hours afterward and imparting a bitter taste to anything I might eat did not diminish my tremendous feeling of importance.

Next I was allowed to fill bright yellow boxes with boracic acid or Epsom salts and label them accordingly. And every Saturday morning it was my job to mix and bottle the citrate of magnesia.

This was an absorbing process, and I immediately imagined myself a famous woman chemist as I measured into the graduate so many ounces of the citric-acid solution, so much simple syrup, so much aqua distillati. The bottles were then corked and labeled.

When sold, we would add the potassium bicarbonate tablet and then seal the bottle with a metal cap. The corks were put back into a special box to be used over again next Saturday.

Mr. Schiller was patient with me, and very kind, but fussy about details such as saving the magnesia corks, putting labels on straight, and never wasting paper or string. Also, alas, about his young clerk sampling the candy bars. Privately, I considered this to be carrying thrift too far. Didn't he have a whole showcase full — *full* of Hershey bars, Tootsie Rolls, and those perfect, luscious things called Hoeffler's Centennials?

My hours in the drugstore soon became my whole existence. I arrived early and stayed late. I learned so many things. About the bottle of hydrocyanic acid that was kept locked up because just one whiff of it could kill a person. How to mark the merchandise with the queer symbols that showed how much each item had cost wholesale. I learned how to make change and the rudiments of salesmanship. If someone bought a washcloth, you immediately showed them the new soap display. Should they purchase calomel, you automatically fixed and wrapped up a bottle of citrate of magnesia so that they would not become something called "salivated," which had to do with teeth getting black and falling out.

It was not long until I was sure that I knew everything.

Then I was trusted to stay alone in the store while Mr. Schiller went home to a hot lunch. From one until two o'clock every afternoon *I* was Schiller's drugstore, and telephoned to Mr. Schiller's home only if a prescription came in.

Carmelita fell into the habit of coming by to visit with me during this hour. If a customer came in, Carmelita would pretend to be buying a magazine. We worked up quite a routine.

"Look through the racks again, madam," I would say to her in a businesslike tone. "Perhaps you will find one you like better. I will be right back, madam, just as soon as I've waited on this customer."

When alone again, we would resume our conversation, leaning idly on the candy counter, Carmelita in front, I at the back. For the first week we contented ourselves with gazing at the gorgeous display, choosing mentally the kinds of candy we would buy if we had five dollars.

Sometimes the whole hour would be spent in this way. Always, though, our imaginary purchases contained a majority of Hoeffler's Centennials. They were Carmelita's favorites as well as mine. Creamy, delicately rum-flavored, one perfect chocolate in a brown cardboard box. Other candies might be larger, we conceded, might give you more for your money — but, ah, there was something so infinitely rich and satisfying about the Centennials' expensive elegance!

If Carmelita or I possessed a nickel, we would purchase one and share it, I conscientiously ringing up the sale on the cash register. If we didn't have a nickel, we would just gaze.

But not for long. Came the day when we took two whole Centennials out of the case and ate them! By devious ways we had arrived at a compromise with our consciences.

First, two little old candy bars among so many would hardly be missed, would they? Then too didn't I work overtime almost every day? Without any pay? Didn't Carmelita devote her time to coming up and staying with me?

Of course Mr. Schiller was old-fashioned and probably wouldn't approve of his clerk's having company during working hours — but what about Mrs. Schiller's constant dread of holdups? Certainly, we assured each other, it was far safer that the two of us be there in the store. If a robber came in, Carmelita could run for a policeman while I pretended I didn't know how to open the register.

We comfortably concluded that Carmelita was practically insurance for Schiller's drugstore, and it was no more than right that she and I should be paid one — perhaps two — Hoeffler Centennials daily.

However, the concrete evidence of our self-administered pay became a problem. We couldn't put the empty boxes into the waste-paper basket, because Mrs. Schiller had a peculiar habit of inspecting that at every opportunity. We couldn't throw the boxes out into the street, because Mr. Schiller swept the sidewalk in front of the store several times a day, and we didn't want him to start wondering at the sudden and brisk sale in candy.

We finally solved the disposal problem by tossing the empty boxes up into the dark recess over the big street window, the one that had the big colored jars in it. A perfect hiding place, we assured each other.

Perfect, that is, until the Saturday the window dresser came to change the window decorations and climbed up to the cubbyhole to get the pink crepe paper he'd stored there the month before.

"Hey, Schiller," I heard him yell, "what you collecting these empty Hoeffler boxes for?"

He began to toss them down, one by one. Dusty, some of them. Crumpled or whole. Before my horrified eyes descended a cloud of empty candy boxes.

I moaned softly. Oh, surely Carmelita and

I had never in the world consumed *that* many! Time stopped, along with my heart, while I watched the growing evidence of my guilt.

I looked up once at Mr. Schiller's surprised but still kind face. I gulped noisily, and he might have spoken, but some evil wind took that moment to blow Mrs. Schiller in through the front door, and from then on nobody else had a chance to speak.

Her tight little eyes took in the situation immediately. Her voice rose and fell in scathing denunciation, and 'the ugly words made me shiver. No one — ever — had talked to me like that, and the next few minutes became the most desolate of my life.

It was as if her tongue had been dipped in the acid that Mr. Schiller kept in a rubber-topped bottle on the back of the shelf because a drop of it could sear off your flesh.

Mrs. Schiller's most frequent — and mildest — word was Thief. Thief, capitalized and set in big screaming letters.

I was not only a dirty, rotten, sneaking, low-down thief that should be sent to the Juvenile Delinquency Court, but I was no good, never would be any good, and nobody in the whole world would ever trust me again.

Mrs. Schiller said so. Mrs. Schiller said so again and again and louder and louder, until in pity for us both, Mr. Schiller made her go to the back of the store.

He finally let me go, and I rushed home to Mama, sobbing wretchedly, carrying the newspaper-wrapped package of empty Hoeffler boxes that Mrs. Schiller had commanded me to take to her.

It was some time before Mama could understand what I tried to tell her. Even then she did not seem to grasp the full import of my degradation, because she only said, "First, you must stop sobbing so, my Katrin."

Her words were so loving, I had to weep anew. Poor, poor Mama, to have such a child as I. A disgrace. A — a thief!

Mama dampened the towel by the sink and wiped my face, holding the coolness against my aching head.

"There now," she said, "there now."

And big girl though I was, she made me sit in her lap while she rocked me gently.

Haltingly, I told her of my crime. And when I got to the part about Mrs. Schiller, she stopped rocking and just held me — tight.

I waited for Mama's answer. Mama could be strict, even stern, when we children had done wrong. I knew that I had sinned dreadfully, and now it was only right and just that I be punished.

Mama stood up so quickly I almost fell. She walked over to the sink and took a drink of water. Her back was so straight, so rigid, I started to cry again.

"Oh, please," I begged. "Please, Mama, don't you be angry too."

She turned and hurried to me, took my shaking hands in hers.

"Not with you, Katrin," she said earnestly. "It is with — but, yes, that can wait. Now — look at me, Daughter."

I looked into her quiet face, watched her mouth try to smile.

"This is important, my Katrin. Perhaps I cannot explain it so well, but you must not ever feel here — " she touched me — "in your heart, that you are what you said. A — a thief. A bad girl."

"But, Mama, I did take them — and Mrs. Schiller said — "

"Katrin, believe me, you are not a thief. You are a good girl."

I shook my head.

"You have been foolish, yes, you have done wrong. But no great wrong. You are still so young—so greedy for sweets, as all young things are."

"Mama, you just don't understand."

"But I do, that is why — " And Mama's laugh rang out suddenly, richly.

I stared at her, "Mama! You laughed!"

"As you must laugh, Daughter. Unless you — " Mama seemed to search for words — "unless you cripple something inside of you.

Something that makes you lift your head after
you have made a mistake. Something that
makes you go on — with — with pride, Katrin."

I lowered my head. "But, Mama," I whispered, "whenever I think of it, oh, Mama, I am
so ashamed!"

"Is good to be ashamed," Mama said briskly. "That makes it sure you will not do such a
thing again. But cannot you see, Katrin, that
with the shame and the sorrow there must
also be the saving laughter?"

"I — I guess so."

"Listen, Daughter, let me tell you why I understand, why I laughed. When Papa was
courting me, I lived, as you know, with your
Aunt Jenny. Every Sunday evening Papa came
to call. We did not have much money, but
somehow Jenny could always contrive refreshments. Cookies, or a cake.

"Once she was able to make a fancy cake
and pile it high with rich white frosting. It
was, I believe, the most beautiful cake I had
ever seen. I was young — it seemed that never did I get enough of sweets — "

Mama's eyes were misty, remembering.

"Well," she continued, "I kept tasting the
frosting, sneaking into Jenny's pantry for just
one more bite, until — oh, Katrin — until
I'd eaten every speck of frosting on that
cake!"

115

I found myself laughing with Mama at the story.

"Then what happened?"

"Jenny was cross, and with reason. So she served the cake that night and told Papa exactly why it looked so bare."

"And what did Papa do?"

Mama smiled a secret smile. "He married me," she said, "anyhow."

I leaned against Mama, relaxed, comforted.

Mama touched my cheek. "So can you smile now," she asked, "and believe that this — this thing you have done is not the end of the world? That you can go on without a voice in your heart ever crying 'Thief'?"

I nodded. "My goodness, though, wasn't I — "

"Foolish," Mama supplied. "And very naughty. And you must pay for the candy you ate. But you are not — *bad.*"

"No, Mama, I guess I'm not *bad.*"

"Is good. Now, you will peel the potatoes for dinner and set the table, I — " Mama's gentle voice hardened — "*I* have a call to make."

And Mama wasn't smiling a bit as she marched out the door.

12 ❧ *Mama's Aunt Elna*

For once, Aunt Trina knew some family gossip before Aunt Jenny did, and she made the most of it. She wouldn't come right out and say what it was; she just dropped little hints, shook her head sadly, and from time to time sighed "Poor, *poor* old Aunt Elna."

The Aunts were all sitting around our kitchen table having coffee with Mama, and I made the drying of the lunch dishes last a long time, so that I would have an excuse to stay and hear their talk. I was eager to hear anything that had to do with my Great-aunt Elna; her tragic story had always enthralled me.

But Aunt Jenny pretended that she didn't hear Aunt Trina's hints, and kept the conversation on other matters. When Aunt Marta tried to question Aunt Trina, Jenny raised her voice and demanded that the sugar be passed.

That was the way Aunt Jenny was. Whenever she disapproved of someone (and she and her mother's sister had quarreled bitterly in times gone by), she simply refused to hear any discussion of that person. While the rest of the Aunts "tsk, tsked" just as loudly about their Aunt Elna as Jenny did, I think that in their hearts they were a little proud, though frightened, at having such a violent character in the family.

This day too Aunt Jenny was particularly cross because she was having so many worries about her big boardinghouse out on Haight Street. Here she'd gone deep into debt to buy new kitchen equipment — had even had Uncle Ole and Papa and Uncle Peter enlarge the dining room and kitchen of her house — but instead of getting and keeping new boarders, she was losing the old ones.

But I had heard all that before, and now I was anxious that Aunt Trina be allowed to tell her news of my Great-aunt Elna.

What could it be? Surely there wasn't much else that *could* happen to her. Though Aunt Elna was very old now, and deaf, she remained a storybook figure to us children. The few times we saw her, we would stare unblinkingly, trying, as we looked at the straight, spare figure, the gray hair pulled uncompromisingly back from the stern face, to discover some trace of the wild young girl who had driven, they said, her false lover to his death.

There was little enough of drama in our lives, and we treasured every colorful detail we could glean about Great-aunt Elna. The story — spoken quickly in Norwegian, so that

118

we children could not readily understand, or told in a hushed, shocked voice when we were considered out of hearing — was as exciting as any saga.

And this was the way the Aunts told it:

The young Elna (and their own mother had told them thusly) had been darkly beautiful, but as wild and headstrong as the sea that seemed caught in her narrow green eyes.

Ever rebellious, flaunting her elders, scornful of all that was seemly, she was betrothed to Peder, son of Lars.

And oh (my grandmother had told the Aunts), despite the clacking and the mutterings of the older folk, the love of Elna and Peder had been a thing to see. Never quiet, you understand, never a gentle thing; more like a storm over the fjords, or a high and pounding wind. They quarreled as often as they kissed and vowed undying hatred as quickly as they plighted their troth anew.

"Troll-ridden," my grandmother had said of them sadly. "Troll-ridden."

They loved horses, the young Elna and the tall Peder. And in a day when maidens stayed properly at home, one that was ever ready to fling herself onto the back of the wildest horse to race her lover over the narrow rocky paths would naturally be expected to come to a bad end. Not that Elna minded ever what the old ones said. As she and Peder galloped by, she was like as not to laugh and mock at their shocked faces.

Perhaps it was meet and just, then, that their final, most terrible quarrel was to be about a horse that Peder had newly bought, a white stallion called Thor that Elna begged to ride.

Peder refused (and rightly so, my grandmother thought), because the horse was still too wild — had never been properly broken.

Elna, they said, raged and shouted that ride him she *would*.

Then indeed had Peder sworn at her, and shouted that likely her spirit needed breaking as badly as Thor's.

And one word led to another and they parted in bitterness.

And Peder went to Oslo — Christiania, then — and loud hissed the gossip when he returned to his homeplace within the week — with a wife.

A rabbity-looking creature, the neighbors reported to Elna, watching her out of the corners of their eyes. Gentle-seeming, though, they added slyly, and ever solicitous of her scowling bridegroom.

Elna held her head high. "Then surely must I pay my respects," was all she said.

And though her parents tried to stop her and her sisters begged and wept, the white-faced girl arrayed herself in the gown that was to have been her wedding dress and bound her long, dark hair. (This, though a small thing, was in itself an affront to God-fearing, respectable folk. Because it was an old custom in that part of the country for a girl to keep her hair unbound until she had been made a wife.)

Dressed in such manner, and holding all her betrothal gifts carefully in front of her, Elna had ridden her mare the miles to Peder's home.

The guests who had gathered to greet the young couple stopped their chattering to stare at Elna as she walked into Peder's place that night and laid Peder's gifts in front of his bride.

"For you," Elna said proudly. "These too I give to you."

And Peder had raged and sworn. It was not seemly, he shouted, that she should act thus. And forbade his wife to touch the gifts.

And Peder's bride tossed her head and taunted Elna. "What need have I of gifts? *I* have Peder."

But Elna's eyes were searching Peder's face, and what she saw there must have been the reason for the strange smile that twisted her mouth. "Have you?" she asked softly, answering Peder's wife. "Have you Peder?"

Elna turned then, and with tall dignity walked out of Peder's house, and perhaps the wedding guests were disappointed that there was to be no more of a scene than that. They stood around awkwardly, each one waiting for his neighbor to break the silence. They heard Elna speak softly to her mare, heard the mare whinny in reply, and stole quick little glances at Peder's unhappy face.

Then all in one second, so it seemed, they heard the new sound, that of heavy and thundering hoofbeats, and when Peder threw open the door, they saw Elna racing down the road that led to the fjord — riding the stallion Thor.

And her only answer to Peder's frantic call was her high and reckless laugh.

In just the time it takes to draw a breath Peder flung himself onto the back of Elna's waiting mare and rode headlong in pursuit.

What happened then was never truly told, because no one knew. (Except, perhaps, Elna, and she was never to speak of that night again.) Whether the mare stumbled, or a strap had been loosened — all that was known was that in some manner Peder was thrown against the jagged rocks that lined the roadway, and died in a minute.

They said that Elna came riding back alone, the stallion stepping high and nervously but doing her bidding. Elna led her mare with Peder's still body across the saddle. She handed the reins to the staring bride and quietly, almost kindly, did she say: "Now, truly, indeed, do you have Peder."

That was the way the Aunts told the story.

The rest wasn't interesting. It was just that Elna's parents sent her to America, and she worked for years for a caterer on Mission Street and got older and grimmer and paid but brief visits to her sister and her sister's children. So that it was not often that we had news of her.

I was doing the last of the silverware when Aunt Jenny stood up and said that she must go. I was secretly glad; now Aunt Trina could tell the news.

I was disappointed.

The news was only that old Aunt Elna was to be taken to the old people's home.

The Aunts, though, and Mama, were shocked and dismayed.

How could this be? they asked. Hadn't Aunt Elna saved money all the time she worked?

Yes, Aunt Trina said. But since she had become so deaf, she was unable to work, and the money had gone to doctors who had tried vainly to cure her deafness. Aunt Elna could read lips, Aunt Trina said, but only if Norwegian were spoken.

"But we must *do* something," Mama said.

The Aunts agreed, and explored the subject endlessly. Each one was more than willing to offer their aunt a home — but would she accept? They remembered her stiff, unyielding pride.

I lost interest. It was, I knew, a terrible thing to have someone even remotely connected to you to have to go to an *institution*, but even I knew that Great-aunt Elna would accept that before she would take family charity. So what could a person do about it?

I reckoned without Mama.

The next day was Saturday, and when I came down the breakfast dishes were piled in the sink and Mama was lying down in her room, but she didn't look a bit sick.

"Fix your breakfast," she told me, "then take Dagmar and go out and play."

I was too startled to be happy about getting out of all the Saturday work. "But, Mama! What about changing the beds? What about sweeping the hall stairs? What about these dishes?"

Mama smiled. "Just leave them. This morning I am going to have company."

Then I was sure that Mama must be sick. *Company* coming and a cluttered, unswept house?

"My Aunt Elna," Mama explained. And I began to understand.

But I took a long time getting my breakfast,

so I was there when my Great-aunt walked in.

Mama apologized for the look of the house, and told me to make fresh coffee. "And make plenty, Katrin."

Aunt Elna looked at Mama with her piercing eyes. "Again?" she demanded sharply. Mama blushed, but shook her head.

"Five children is enough," Great-aunt Elna declared in her flat voice, and she sat down in the chair that faced Mama's bed.

"Now why else," she wondered, "would you be lying in bed with work undone?"

Mama took a deep breath and started to speak, but Aunt Elna stopped her.

"Don't bother," she said grimly. "You were never able to lie. I was to feel that I was needed here, and so would come and live with you?"

Mama nodded.

Aunt Elna snorted. "Understand, I appreciate your offer — but I will take the — the other."

"Please," Mama pleaded, "we would make you happy here —"

Aunt Elna shook her head vigorously. "You have little enough to do with, and two great girls to help you do the work. I would be a — burden."

Mama spoke then of Marta, of Sigrid, of Trina — but old Aunt Elna wouldn't listen. "I want none of it," she declared. "I want just to go my own way the time I have left." Her thin mouth twisted. "Too long a time, perhaps. Unfortunately, I come from a long-lived family."

Mama sat up in bed and reached for Aunt Elna's hand, but Aunt Elna snatched it away. "Look," Mama said eagerly, "perhaps, then, we can find work for you to do. You are strong — "

"And who," demanded Aunt Elna, "would take a woman past seventy — stone-deaf? An old woman who cannot sleep at night and needs must walk the streets for hours at a time to tire herself sufficiently so that she can catch but winks of sleep? No. I am tired of people, tired of trying to hear what they shout at me. If I could work alone — be alone — why speak of it? It is impossible."

But Mama wouldn't give up. "If we do," she insisted, "if we do find some sort of job, you would take it?"

For just a second, Aunt Elna's face crumpled. "I," she said softly, "I would do almost anything, rather than the — other." Then she made her back very straight and stood up. "It is foolish to hope, I have learned," she said shortly. "Come now, get out of that bed and I will help you clear up the kitchen before I — I go."

"Make some of your gingerbread," Mama said. "I must go to the store."

Great-aunt Elna was a wonderful cook. She

made a batch of her famous Danish pastry. It was rising by the stove, her gingerbread was in the oven, and she was pressing out the fancy cookies that were Papa's favorites, when Aunt Jenny walked in.

When she saw her Aunt Elna there, she almost turned to walk out of the kitchen. "So," she said sternly to Mama, "this is why you phoned to me?"

Mama went over and took hold of Aunt Jenny's arm. "You will sit down," she said quietly, "and hear what I have to say. You too," she said to Aunt Elna, who had started to put on her coat.

"I cannot hear you," Aunt Elna said flatly.

"Look at me, then," Mama said. "And you, Jenny, listen before you answer."

Mama poured out three cups of coffee and made Aunt Jenny and Great-aunt Elna sit down to the table.

"Now." Mama took a deep breath. "First, we must remember that we are all of the same family."

"I want no help from any of you," Great-aunt Elna said loudly and suddenly.

"But," Mama said quietly, "one of us wants help from *you*."

Great-aunt Elna looked interested, Aunt Jenny wary.

"So," Mama said. "So here is Jenny, widowed and alone, losing all that she has put into her boardinghouse because — wait, Jenny, let me speak out — because she is a very poor cook."

I gulped at Mama's daring and watched Aunt Jenny's face darken with anger.

"I don't cook so bad," Aunt Jenny protested. "My meats — my gravies — "

"Poor Jenny works night and day," Mama went on serenely, "seeking to save her business. She has made room for twenty-three boarders, but has only — what is it now, Jenny?"

"Five," Aunt Jenny said unwillingly.

"So," Mama said. "And here is Aunt Elna, who would rather cook than do anything else, who is the finest cook I know — making plans to spend her days among strangers and in unhappiness."

"Have you, then, lost your wits?" Aunt Jenny cried. "No one knows better than you how little we are able to get along, Aunt Elna and I."

"A hundred times better the strangers," Great-aunt Elna shouted, "than to work for such as Jenny!"

"Never!" Aunt Jenny shouted back. "Never!"

Mama stirred her coffee calmly. "I have figured it all out. You would not even see each other. That little room off your kitchen, Jenny, you could give that to Aunt Elna."

Great-aunt Elna started thumping on the table in disagreement, but Mama went right on talking. "Aunt Elna cannot sleep at night, so she will do her work then. You, Jenny, after the dinner dishes are done, will leave the kitchen and not come back. You will have all that will be needed in the pantry and Aunt Elna will do the baking. The bread, the pies, the cakes, and the doughnuts will all be baked at night. By dawn, Aunt Elna will leave the kitchen, and you, Jenny, will take over."

"Aunt Elna," Mama continued, "will have what she wants: quiet, work, and independence. You, Jenny, will soon have a boarding-house that will be famous for its good cooking, and more boarders than you will have room for."

Great-aunt Elna and my Aunt Jenny stared at Mama and then at each other. In the silence, Mama drank her coffee.

It was Aunt Jenny who spoke first. "I do not say that such help as that, at this time, would not be God-sent — but — but — "

Great-aunt Elna spoke grudgingly. "Would be good to have a kitchen to myself again. There is a new roll recipe — "

Aunt Jenny unbent a little more. "Never have I said that Aunt Elna was not a fine cook."

Great-aunt Elna: "Always have I said Jenny worked harder than anyone I knew."

129

"For such help as that," Jenny said fairly, "I could pay a little as well as giving room and board."

"A person could also put up the lunches for the men," Great-aunt Elna offered.

Mama stood up briskly. "So," she said. "So it is settled, then. Jenny, you will have Aunt Elna's room ready. Papa will bring her over this evening."

"Why," Jenny said, "that won't be necessary. We can go now and get things settled. We can go — together."

And Mama's eyes began to dance. "Is good," she said gravely. "Is very good."

13 ❧ Mama
and Uncle Elizabeth

Our next-door neighbor, Mrs. Karboe, gave Dagmar a cat.

A fierce, independent little cat that arched its back and spat vindictively at the slightest provocation.

It was love at first sight. On Dagmar's part, at least. She took one long look and immediately forsook dolls, jacks, and the little boy next door.

"Elizabeth," she crooned. "My Elizabeth."

And from that day forward she carried Elizabeth with her wherever she went. Elizabeth mutinied often, especially when she was forced to ride in the doll carriage, and Dagmar's scratched arms bore testimony to the arguments the two of them must have had.

Christine and I tried to stop the almost constant companionship. We even appealed to Mama.

"First thing you know," Christine said, "she'll have the darned cat sleeping with her."

Dagmar looked interested.

"Oh, my goodness," Aunt Jenny said, "that would never do! Why, everyone knows that a cat draws breath from a sleeping child." She turned to Dagmar. "How would you like to wake up some morning *smothered*?" she asked.

Dagmar looked stubborn. "I wouldn't care! Elizabeth can have *all* my breath." She picked up the uncooperative kitten and blew earnestly into its face. "There! And there! And there!"

Elizabeth spat furiously and Mama made Dagmar stop.

"Besides," Christine said loftily, " 'Elizabeth' is a very silly name for a cat."

Dagmar held the struggling beast close to her and faced us defiantly. "She is my Elizabeth," she cried with the full passion of her eight years. "She loves me! Even if she doesn't show it — in front of people. 'N Elizabeth is a bee-yoo-tiful name and I'm going to name all her kittens 'Elizabeth' — so there!"

Well, Elizabeth grew older, but no more mellowed. Her disposition became, if possible, even meaner, and her vocabulary consisted entirely of cat expletives. And very soon it became evident that Elizabeth was not the kind of a cat that had kittens named Elizabeth.

Elizabeth, in short, was a tomcat. A wild, fighting, irascible, look-for-trouble tomcat that turned our friendly neighbors into bitter enemies.

In deference to Dagmar — who still insisted upon the "Elizabeth" — the cat became, for name-calling purposes, "Uncle Elizabeth."

As Uncle Elizabeth waxed lean and strong, the scars and marks of his ceaseless backfence battles multiplied. First he lost the tip of one ear, then practically the whole of the other. His back was striped with bald spots where one or another of his enemies had taken a cat nip. It became the accepted thing for Uncle Elizabeth to have at least one eye constantly swollen shut.

Mama fretted, but Dagmar just put on her white apron, and with firm gentleness — which consisted of sitting on him — bathed the weary warrior's wounds with boric-acid solution.

But at last came the day when even Dagmar's medical ingenuity failed. Uncle Elizabeth limped home one dawn with half a paw chewed off, a walnut-sized lump on the side of his head, both eyes swollen shut, and one-fourth of his tail missing.

He mewed plaintively, and told us in no uncertain terms that if he just lived through this debacle, he would be content to stay at home forever after. But all his good intentions, and Dagmar's careful nursing, went for naught.

With suppurating wounds and swollen head, Uncle Elizabeth became a dreadful and terrible sight.

Dagmar's despair was heartbreaking. When Nels and I could stand it no longer, we gave her fifty cents to take him to the veterinary's.

"And listen," Christine said. "If he can't do anything for the poor thing, tell him to put it out of its misery."

Dagmar's lips tightened stubbornly, but she took the money.

Within an hour she was back, still clutching Uncle Elizabeth, and the half-dollar. "He's no doctor!" she yelled indignantly. "He says my beautiful, darling cat is practically dead now."

Mama took the cat away from Dagmar. "This has gone far enough," she scolded gently. "Would it not be better for the poor thing to go quietly to sleep?"

"No!"

"But he is suffering, Dagmar."

"No, Mama, no! Make him live, Mama. Make him well again. *Please.*"

Mama turned away from the pleading eyes and put the cat in the big box on the back porch. "Scrub your hands good," she told Dagmar.

"Are you going to fix Uncle Elizabeth, Mama? Are you going to make him well for me?"

"But, Dagmar, little Daughter, if even a doctor could not help him — "

"Please, Mama, say that you will make him well for me."

Mama started to speak, then turned away. "Let us see how the cat gets through the night," she said. "You go to bed now."

But as we sat around the table late that night and listened to the mournful howls, it didn't look as if any of us could get through the night.

"If only Papa were here," Mama said. "He would know what to do."

But Papa had gone to a union meeting and would not be home until very late.

Mama looked at the rest of us. "Do any of you know what to do?"

We shook our heads.

"Oh, the *poor* thing," Mama said, as a wilder, more dismal howl reached our ears, "he is in agony. If he must die anyhow — will one of you — ?"

We shook our heads more vigorously, and Christine said that she had heard that chloroform was good.

Mama stood up. "It is the only kind thing to do," she said. And sent Christine to the drugstore for a bottle of chloroform.

Mama gave Uncle Elizabeth a prodigious last supper of cream, tucked him gently into his bed, and proceeded to turn it into a lethal chamber.

First, she moistened the big sponge with all the chloroform and put it into the box with Uncle Elizabeth, and then piled sacks and blankets on top of the box. There wasn't a sound from the interior — not even one last mournful mew.

We watched with admiration.

"I don't envy you your job in the morning, Mama," I said. "Having to tell Dagmar."

Mama nodded sadly. "Poor little girl."

The next morning, Dagmar's face was sunny with anticipation when she burst into the kitchen. "Is Uncle Elizabeth all better yet, Mama?"

Mama tried to take Dagmar on her lap. "Daughter," she said gently, "there is something I must tell you."

But Dagmar had danced away to the box that held all that was left of Uncle Elizabeth. She took off the blankets and sacks, one by one. "My goodness," she said, "did you think he'd catch cold?"

Mama appealed to Papa in an anxious whisper. "Tell her. Do something."

Dagmar leaned over the box. "What a funny, funny smell. Good morning, my darling, my dear, my Elizabeth."

And out of the box she lifted a sleepy,

yawning Uncle Elizabeth! A truly resurrected Uncle Elizabeth! Both eyes were open; the dreadful swelling on the head had gone down, and the wounds were clean and dry.

Dagmar set the miracle down on the floor, then threw herself into Mama's arms. "I *knew* you would fix him," she sobbed, the pent-up tears crowding down her cheeks. "I *knew* you would make him well."

"But, Dagmar, I didn't. Please listen — "

But Dagmar was too busy whispering words of love to the sleepy Lazarus.

"Papa," Mama said to him. "Papa, you tell her."

"A cat," Papa said, "has nine lives. Besides, you probably did not use enough chloroform."

"But it is not *good*," Mama protested, "to let her grow up believing that I can fix everything."

Papa touched Mama's hand. "Leave her alone," he advised. "She will learn the sad things soon enough. Besides — " and Papa chuckled deep in his throat — "besides, I know *exactly* how Dagmar feels."

By the end of the year we had seven boarders. The Stanton brothers had brought us Mr. Lewis and Mr. Clark, who made jokes about their names and said they were explorers. They weren't, really; they were bookkeepers for the Gas and Electric Company.

And Professor Jannough and his wife had moved into the two big side rooms and used them for a piano studio. The shaggy professor could play the piano something wonderful, and little Mrs. Jannough would often sing for us in Polish.

The older Stanton brother, Sam, had finally got Miss Durant to like steak, medium rare, and he and Miss Durant became engaged. After June, when they got married, they were going to take the big downstairs room and give Mr. George Miss Durant's upstairs room.

I was in high now and Nels was a senior, and even talking about going over to the university across the bay. Christine was graduating from Winford, and she was so smart she had won the Winford medal for outstanding achievement.

I believe the night that Christine graduated was one of the proudest for Mama and Papa. Mama put the shiny medal in a velvet-lined box she had, and kept it in her bureau drawer. Kept it there when she wasn't showing it to all the boarders, to the Aunts and the Uncles, even to Mr. Tree, the groceryman.

We naturally expected Christine to go on to high.

To Mama and Papa an education was the finest thing in the world, and unlike other parents we knew they did not consider it a sacrifice to keep us all in school.

But Christine — without a word to any of us — went downtown and got herself a job in the overall factory. She wasn't willful about it, just very matter-of-fact.

"I want clothes," she said reasonably, "and other things."

Vainly Mama and Papa pointed out the advantages of high school.

"No," she said. "No, thank you."

Christine wouldn't even say that she would go on to night school. She was quick about learning how to operate the machines, and she said that in a little while she would be just as fast as the other operators, and then she would do piecework and make more money.

It was not an unusual thing for girls to go to work directly after grammar school. In my own class, seven of the girls had not gone on to high. Even my beloved Carmelita had dropped out of Lowell to go to work as stock girl in the five-and-ten.

But Christine! Whose grades were always the highest — who had won a medal! Nels and I had worked, of course, but only during school vacation.

Mama pleaded and pleaded, but it didn't do any good. Christine remained serene and calm — but she kept on working. It was the first time one of us children had deliberately gone against Mama and Papa, and it was a strange and saddening thing.

I could not understand how Christine could hold out against the grief in Mama's eyes. But she did, going her own quiet way, getting up early to fix her own lunch, taking the street-car to work.

She brought her first week's pay home and put it on the kitchen table. "It is for you," she said to Mama.

Mama looked at the heap of coins and shook her head sadly.

"I do not want it, Christine."

"What's wrong with it, Mama? It's honest money. I worked hard for it."

Mama shook her head again. "It is not good money. It is taking away from you your youngness, your chance at an education. Better that you forget the job, my Christine, and go on to high with Katrin and Nels."

But Christine only shut her lips stubbornly and left the money right on the table. And since Mama wouldn't touch it, it stayed right there. When I cleared and washed the table, I went around the money.

The money in the center of the table put a pall on all our lives. No one ever spoke of it, but always it lay there — a symbol of something that had gone wrong in the family.

I tried to tell Mama it wasn't any use. Christine would always have her own way in the end, but Mama wouldn't listen.

One week's — two weeks' — wages piled up on the table.

Then Mama bought Christine the red plaid dress. Out of money from the Little Bank.

"Always have you wanted the red dress." Mama offered it eagerly.

Christine touched the rich folds, and might have weakened. But just then Mama pointed out how warm the dress was, how serviceable. "Just what the other girls are wearing at high now."

Christine put the dress back in the box and didn't say a word.

And Mama knew she had failed.

The third week's wages were added to the pile, and it was like a weight upon us. No more laughter and little jokes as we sat around the table doing our homework. Christine was so tired at night she went directly to bed, and her empty chair seemed to shout the fact that our family circle was broken — askew.

Papa had had lots of overtime work, and he said that the extra money was for Mama to get herself a coat.

"Always," he said, "something happens when you go to buy the coat. This time, sure, you must buy for yourself."

Mama said that she would.

We all made suggestions. Dagmar and I said that the coat must have fur — even a little — on the collar; Nels said that he liked a dark-brown color; and Papa insisted that above all else it must be warm. Only Christine said nothing.

I came home early from school the next day to take care of little Kaaren, so that Mama would have plenty of time to pick out her coat.

Mama was unusually late in getting home. Papa and Nels had come in — even Christine. Dagmar and I set the table in the dining room for the boarders, added wood to the stove, and cut the bread.

We had almost begun to worry when Mama finally came into the kitchen, almost staggering under a heavy, bulky package.

"The coat!" Dagmar cried. "Let us see the new coat."

"Well, now, I will tell you," Mama said slowly — and we knew that she had not bought the coat.

Nels opened the heavy package and in silence took out twelve big books and stacked them on the table.

"Complete High School Course," he read, "In Twelve Easy-to-Read Volumes."

"For Christine," Mama explained. "She will get the fine education right at home by studying nights." Mama smiled at Christine. "You will do that for Mama?"

Christine bit her lip and looked at us helplessly.

She touched the books. "You spent your coat money for these?"

Mama shrugged. "The coat I can get another time. But these — Christine?"

Christine smiled and looked right at Mama. "Tomorrow," Christine said, "tomorrow I will go to high with Nels and Kathryn."

We all started talking at once, and Dagmar's voice was the loudest. "What," she demanded, "are you going to do with that old money on the table?"

Christine giggled and swept the money up and put it in the Little Bank. "For furniture," she said, "and more boarders."

Mama sat down in the rocking chair and took little Kaaren into her arms. The kitchen was warm and comfortable, Uncle Elizabeth sang to himself in his box by the stove. The notes of Professor Jannough's piano tinkled into the silence, and we could hear the Stanton brothers and Mr. Lewis and Mr. Clark and Miss Durant talking gaily in the hall.

Mama looked at us and smiled happily.

"Life is good," she said contentedly. "Life is so good."

15 ᘒᴥ *Mama and Papa*

The years that Christine and I spent at Lowell High were good years, for all they flew by so quickly. Our tow-colored hair, by some miracle, had turned a passable golden color, and we discovered that we had nice complexions and attractive teeth. Clothes and school activities became engrossing subjects, and boys were fun to know.

I was finally asked to join the sacrosanct Mummers' Club at school (and wrote reams of plays — most of them tragic — which I insisted upon producing). Christine headed the debating team and the honor society, and Nels was in his fourth year of pre-med at the university across the bay.

Our baby Kaaren had become a solemn, lovable treasure of six, and sturdy Dagmar spent her days in collecting stray dogs and cats and her nights in ministering to them.

Little by little, the foreignness had disappeared almost entirely from our family life. Only on special occasions did Mama make the lutefisk or fladbröd, and she and Papa seldom spoke Norwegian anymore. They had learned to play whist, and went often to neighborhood card parties or to shows.

But the Steiner Street house remained home in every sense of the word. We never even thought of it as a "boardinghouse," because although new boarders came, they stayed on and on to become part of the family.

Two little old ladies, the Misses Jane and Margaret Randolph, now had the sunny back bedroom upstairs, and they told Mama shyly that they had never been so happy in their lives. They were real ladies, the Misses Randolph, and had been belles in the early days of San Francisco, before their dear father had been swindled out of his fortune. They had a tiny income, which they augmented by doing intricate crocheting and beaded bags for the Woman's Exchange.

Then there was big, laughing Mr. Grady, who was a policeman and a widower. He had a fascinating Irish brogue, and every payday he brought Miss Margaret and Miss Jane a box of fancy peppermints from the Pig 'n Whistle. And he never learned that the gentle ladies could not abide the flavor of peppermint, and we young ones never told, because we were the ultimate and grateful consumers.

Papa enclosed the huge basement room in beaverboard, cut windows, and laid a smooth

146

pine floor. Mr. Lewis and Mr. Clark and the Stanton brothers had a great time helping him paint it. Mrs. Sam Stanton, nee Durant, made cushions for the benches Papa built along the wall, and the Misses Randolph sewed fancy shades for all the lamps.

Professor Jannough was able to get an old practice piano, and Mr. Grady contributed his big old-fashioned phonograph.

Nels nicknamed the room the "Glory Hole," and nearly every evening the folks would congregate there to visit, to listen to the phonograph or have the professor play for them, to beg Mrs. Jannough to sing her Polish lullabies.

There too Christine and Nels and I brought our friends and gave our parties. And considered ourselves blessed above all the other young folk we knew, who had to entertain in small apartments or flats.

The newest addition to our group was Mr. Johnny Kenmore and his frail and lovely wife. Mr. Kenmore was that exciting thing, an *aviator,* and every Sunday he took people for airplane rides over the Marina. Whenever he flew, Mrs. Kenmore would come out into the kitchen and sit with Mama until the telephone rang and Mr. Kenmore said he was on his way home.

Papa loved to talk of flying and of air-

147

planes, to hear Mr. Kenmore tell of his many adventures. Papa's eyes would sparkle and shine and he would shake his head in admiration.

"What a wonderful thing," he would marvel. "To fly. To *fly!*"

"It's a great feeling," Mr. Kenmore agreed.

"To fly," Papa said. "High up. Like a bird."

"I'll take you up sometime," Mr. Kenmore offered carelessly one evening. "Any time you say."

Papa sat up eagerly, and I heard Mama catch her breath.

I guess Papa heard her too because he sat back in his chair, and after a while he said, "N-n-no, no, I guess not."

"Oh, come on," Mr. Kenmore coaxed, "you'd love it."

"Would be wonderful," Papa said wistfully. "Just once — to fly."

He looked at Mama again, but her face was bent over her sewing. So Papa said: "Thank you for your offer, Mr. Kenmore, but no. Better, perhaps, that I stay on the ground."

Mr. Kenmore started to speak again, but Mrs. Kenmore stood up quickly and her usually quiet voice was shrill. "Stop urging, Johnny," she cried, *"please."*

So nothing more was said about flying, and Papa didn't mention it again. But I could see that Mama was worried about something. Every once in a while she stole quick little glances at Papa's face, trying, perhaps, to read his thoughts.

One day as I helped her hang out the clothes, she looked up at the sky and said: "This flying, I do not understand it. It is a frightening thing."

When I didn't answer, she continued as if she were thinking out loud, "To want to go so high. So far away."

Mama never served meals to the boarders on Sunday. That was the family's day. One Sunday, Papa and Nels had gone over to the bay to watch the fishermen. Aunt Sigrid and Uncle Peter had taken Dagmar and Kaaren to the park and Christine and I went down to the library to catch up on our homework.

But by five o'clock we had all returned and gathered in the kitchen to wonder why Mama wasn't home and our dinner ready for us.

Just as Papa had decided to telephone Aunt Jenny's to ask if Mama were there, we heard her quick step in the hall. She came into the kitchen in a rush, her cheeks pink and her eyes glowing.

"Papa," she said, "Papa, you must go flying. You must go with Mr. Kenmore next Sunday."

I had never seen Papa look more surprised. "You mean," he said, "that you would not mind?"

"So badly have you wanted to go," Mama said. "And you are right. It is wonderful."

"But how — "

"Oh," Mama said, "I go up today to see if it is safe. Is all right now for you to go."

And Mama could not understand why Papa and the rest of us laughed until we cried.

One of Mama's dreams had been realized at last.

We had enough boarders so that all the leaves must be put in the dining room table.

With the coming of Mr. and Mrs. Sully, who worked in offices downtown, and of the dark and vivid Miss Bartlett, who taught art in a private school, we had fifteen boarders.

Although the boardinghouse made money now and Papa worked steadily, the old and thrifty ways continued. The Little Bank was full these days, and Mama explained to us how the money would be used. So much for Christine, who wanted to be a nurse; so much for Katrin when she went on to normal to learn to be a teacher; so much to help Nels establish his practice when his doctor's training would be finished.

Nels was interning at the City and County Hospital, and had just one night a week and Sunday afternoons off. We were all so proud of Nels. He was a great favorite with the boarders too, and joked and laughed with them when they declared they were just holding back their illnesses until he could take care of them.

Mama's and Papa's eyes would light up whenever they spoke of the time that Nels would be that wonderful person, a *doctor*. To them, it was a never-ending miracle that a child of theirs had achieved such a marvelous thing.

"Just think," Mama would say. "He will be able to help people who are ill. He will save lives."

"He might even," Dagmar boasted, "become famous."

Mama shook her head. "To be famous is not important. But to be able to stop pain — to know how to do so much good — "

I do not know how we learned that Nels was in love with the beautiful and social Cora Martin and that she wanted him to go into her family's business so that they could get married.

First, I remember overhearing Mama tell Papa that she was worried about Nels.

"Maybe he is in love," Papa teased.

But there was no answering smile from Mama. "If he is," she said slowly, "he is finding small joy in it. And that is not good. So sad he is. So troubled."

Then Nels brought Miss Cora Martin to the

house on his next night off. She talked very fast and gushed over Kaaren and said that Dagmar was "quaint" because Dagmar was amazed that Miss Martin had an automobile all her own and could drive it anywhere she pleased.

She called me "Little Sister," and said that she had two brothers, and would give anything in the world if she could blush the way I did.

Miss Martin talked loudly and distinctly to Mama and Papa, as if they could not understand her easily, and she called Nels "Nelson."

"Nels," she said, "is just too, too — imagine introducing anyone as *Nels.*"

Papa tried to explain that only if Nels were the *son* of Nels could he be called "Nels's son." And since Nels had been named for his *grandfather* — but Miss Martin just laughed some more and said that really they must go, and she had so enjoyed meeting us all.

Nels stood up obediently, but his face was strained and tired-looking as he said good night. He would take Miss Martin home, he told Mama, and then go on to the hospital.

Miss Martin sighed. "And that's another thing. The way this stubborn, stubborn boy insists upon slaving for that old M.D. Perhaps — " she held Nels's arm tightly and looked up at him — "perhaps I can make him change his mind."

And even though she laughed, her words sounded firm.

None of us had much to say after Nels and Miss Martin left.

Mama sighed once, then said that we would have to call on Miss Martin's parents. "We will go next Sunday."

Christine looked worried. "Mama, I don't think people do that sort of thing anymore."

"But we are the family of the — the boy," Mama explained. "It is our place to make the — the girl welcome. To meet her parents and become friendly."

So despite Christine's misgivings, on the following Sunday Mama had us dress in our very best clothes and we took the streetcar over to the Sea Cliff district to call on the Martins.

Their house was white and two-storied and surrounded by smooth lawns and a trim and formal rose garden. A Japanese boy in a white coat answered our ring. He asked us to step into the hall, and soon Mrs. Martin came down the polished stairs.

She was pretty too, and talked even faster than her daughter. "Nice of you to call," she murmured, but her eyes were on the watch on her wrist. "Desolated that I did not know. I'm having a little Mah-Jongg party this afternoon; a group of us play together regularly. Fascinating game, Mah-Jongg. Do you play?"

Mama shook her head and made as if to go,

154

but Mrs. Martin said: "We can visit until they come — which won't be for another fifteen minutes. And here is Mr. Martin."

Mr. Martin was small and dark and bitter-looking, but he shook hands heartily with Papa and bowed politely to Mama. "Fine boy you have," he said. "Fine boy, that Nelson."

"Nels," Papa said quietly. "*Nels.*"

"Such a healthy animal," Mrs. Martin said vivaciously. "So strong, so virile. I tell Cora it's a good thing she saw him before I did."

Mama frowned faintly.

Mrs. Martin did not ask us to sit down, so we stood around awkwardly as she asked questions about all of us children.

"Nelson is so proud of you," she told us. "Sometimes I think he puts entirely too much emphasis on family."

"You do not think that is good, Mrs. Martin?" Mama asked.

She shrugged. "I wouldn't know. *I* haven't spoken to my sisters in twenty years."

Just then a little boy peered over the banisters and made a particularly horrid face at us.

"Rupert," Mrs. Martin called. "Rupert darling, come down and meet Nelson's family."

It took five wild minutes to get Rupert down. He yelled and kicked and screamed, and finally hid himself in the velvet portières that lined the windows.

155

"Rupert's a problem child," Mrs. Martin said, as if that explained everything.

"And a spoiled brat," Mr. Martin added. He sounded as if he disliked Rupert intensely.

Then we heard a key in the front door and a handsome young man stumbled in.

Mrs. Martin put her arms around him and said: "You bad, bad boy. Why didn't you phone? I worried all night long."

And Mr. Martin's mouth twisted as he looked at the boy's rumpled clothes and reddened eyes.

"My older son, Edward," Mrs. Martin introduced him. "This is Nelson's family, dear."

Edward mumbled something without looking directly at any of us, and started up the stairs, holding tight to the banister.

"You know how it is with boys," Mrs. Martin said to Mama. "They *will* drink, they *will* run around. But as I always say, just give them enough time, give them enough — "

"Give them enough rope," Mr. Martin interrupted, "and the state will hang 'em for you."

I felt so sorry for Mama and Papa. These people acted so queerly, talked so strangely — as if they were quarreling hatefully beneath all their polite words.

Mrs. Martin smiled thinly and change the subject.

I grew tired of standing, so I leaned against

the wall. I brightened, though, when the Japanese boy wheeled a laden tea tray into the hall. I could see tiny cakes with decorative frosting on their tops, and that big napkin-covered plate *must* be sandwiches.

I caught Christine's eye and nodded, but she only grimaced at me and hissed, "Get out of his way."

I moved away from the wall then, and the servant nodded his thanks as he wheeled the collation past me and into the other room.

Rupert came to life and darted out from the portières and started a high and monotonous shrieking that only subsided when Nels and Miss Cora Martin walked in.

Miss Martin was dressed all in white and she had a white silk band around her head. She greeted us prettily and hung on Nels's arm. Nels did not say much, but I saw him glance into the other room, saw him mark how we all stood in the hall.

Then Mama said that we would have to leave. The fifteen minutes were up, and Mrs. Martin's guests would be arriving. Mama and Papa shook hands with Mr. and Mrs. Martin and Mama asked Nels if he would be home for dinner.

Miss Cora Martin answered for him. "I'm so sorry. We've a date for tennis."

Perhaps, then, Nels suggested quietly, they could drive his folks home?

Cora was sorry again, but there really wasn't time. "The streetcars go regularly," she assured us.

When we got home, Mama and Papa went directly to the kitchen. They closed the door after them, so I hung around the hall unhappily.

I wasn't surprised when I heard Nels's key in the front door.

"Where are they?" he asked me.

"In the kitchen. Making coffee, I think."

"Did they say anything?"

I shook my head.

Nels's mouth tightened. "That was a beautiful exhibition of snobbery today, wasn't it?"

"Christine was right. We shouldn't have gone."

Nels's mouth did not relax. "Have you ever," he demanded, "seen anyone come into this house that Mama and Papa did not make them feel at ease? Make them welcome?"

"No, Nels."

"Have you ever seen them treat anyone as they were treated today?"

"Please, Nels, don't say any more. It will only spoil things for you and Miss Martin."

Nels laughed shortly. "There's nothing more to spoil."

"What do you mean?"

158

"I mean that it's finished. Done with. After you left — "

"But if you are in love with her — "

Nels looked embarrassed. "Look. I'm not. I guess I — I never was. I feel like seven kinds of a fool, but I'm not — you know — in love with her anymore."

I had to smile at his stammering.

"How are you going to tell Mama and Papa?"

"I don't know. But that doesn't bother me nearly as much as how I'm going to explain away what happened to them today. They must be deeply hurt." He took my arm. "Come along in with me, will you? Maybe you can help."

Mama and Papa looked up at us as we came in and they smiled sadly at Nels.

Nels kissed Mama, which was unusual, and he gripped Papa's shoulder tightly.

"Sit down," Papa said quietly. "We have been speaking of you." And he nodded to Mama.

"It is like this," Mama said slowly. "Papa and I — we do not think it would be a good thing for you to marry Miss Martin."

"Look, Mama, if you're thinking about today — "

"Today, Nels? What about today?"

"Why — the way the Martins acted."

159

"Oh, that," Mama said, "*that* does not matter. What *does* matter," she continued earnestly, "is that although they are rich and handsome — the family — forgive me for having to say this, Nels — but the family background — it is not good."

Nels looked as bewildered as I.

"Papa and I," Mama coughed delicately, "were thinking of — of your children."

Nels let out a shout, and then his face got solemn. "I see," he said. "I see what you mean."

Mama looked at him sympathetically, reached out her hand to him. "So if you do not mind too much — "

Nels kept his face straight. "I do not mind," he assured her. "And you and Papa are right. A child — it might be like Rupert." He pretended to shudder.

"Nelson," Papa said suddenly. "*Nelson*."

I giggled at Papa's indignation and he began to laugh too. But Mama did not smile. She was watching Nels's face, looking into his eyes that were clear and happy again.

"Why," she said, "you *do* not mind, do you?"

Nels wrinkled up his nose and grinned at her.

"Good." Mama sighed relievedly. "*Good*."

17 ❧ *Mama*
and the Grandchild

Christine was the first of us to marry.

Frank Shelds was a doctor, a classmate of Nels's, and he and Christine became engaged during the year she was completing her nurse's training.

They were married in the big front parlor by the bay window the Misses Randolph had decorated in white stock and white satin ribbon. Professor Jannough played the wedding march and Mrs. Jannough sang "Oh, Promise Me" so beautifully that both Mrs. Sully and Mr. Grady wept.

Great-aunt Elna baked the towering wedding cake, and all the Aunts helped cook the wedding dinner. Papa and the Uncles gave all the Norwegian toasts they knew, and Mr. Grady told funny Irish stories.

What with friends and boarders and family, there were more than fifty of us to raise our glasses of punch and shout "Skoal!" to the gay young bride and bridegroom.

Christine was beautiful that day.

She and Frank left immediately after the wedding for the little northern town he had chosen to start his practice in.

During the year, we heard from Christine regularly, knew how happy and content she was in her new life, but we did not see her again until Frank brought her down to San Francisco to have her baby.

"Because we knew," Christine said, "that Mama would never forgive us if we allowed her very first grandchild to be born any place else."

But there was something else — something hidden beneath the teasing and the too quick laughter. It was almost as if Christine was — afraid.

I was at school teaching the day they took Christine to the hospital, and when the telephone call came, I got another teacher to take my class and hurried over there.

Mama was waiting for me in the hall.

"They will not let me see her," she said simply.

And her eyes were as stark as they had been on the long-ago day when Dagmar had been wheeled down a hospital corridor away from her — as the time Papa had been so ill.

We waited together outside Christine's door until Nels and Frank came out.

"How is she?" Mama asked anxiously.

Nels shook his head and Frank took hold of both of Mama's hands, as if for comfort.

"But what is *wrong*?"

"Christine believes," Nels said hopelessly, "that she is going to die."

"But — is she?"

Frank looked down at Mama's hands for a long time.

When he looked up, his young face was gaunt. "She is. Unless she gives us some help. Nothing we say — She's not having an easy time. Now she's given up completely."

Mama took her hands out of Frank's and straightened her hat.

"I go in," she said.

"I'm afraid it wouldn't do any good, Mama," Nels said. "It might even be bad for her. One look at your face — "

"Then I will change my face. Like this. See?" Mama smiled valiantly.

Nels put his arm around Mama's shoulder. "No."

"But I'm her Mama."

"And I'm her brother and Frank is her husband. We love Christine too. Believe me, we're doing everything we can. We're doctors."

"Yes," Mama said mildly, "but have you ever had a baby?"

And with that, she marched directly into

163

Christine's room, beckoning me to follow.

Christine's face was white and still against the pillow.

"Mama?"

"Yes, Christine."

"Oh, Mama, will you take my baby — afterwards?" Christine's voice seemed caught in her throat. "We children were so happy, so safe. Mama, will you?"

Mama walked over to the window and raised the shade.

"And what," she wanted to know, "will you be doing while I'm raising your baby?"

Tears coursed down Christine's cheeks. "Didn't they tell you? Don't you know? I — I won't be here."

"And I always thought," Mama said quietly, "that Katrin was the dramatic one."

"Mama! What do you mean?"

"I remember now, Christine, that you are the stubborn one."

Christine buried her face in the pillow. "Oh, you still don't understand. I'm going to die!"

Mama's voice was even. "I had five children. And with every one, I too was certain I was going to die."

"But I *know*. I'm a nurse."

Mama walked over to the bed and looked down at Christine.

"Perhaps," she suggested, "it will be better if you stop being a nurse and start becoming a mother."

Christine closed her eyes and sighed wearily.

A student nurse tiptoed in with a tray. "Though I don't suppose," she whispered compassionately, "that she'll be able to eat a thing."

Christine moaned softly and Mama said, "Please leave the tray anyhow."

After the nurse had gone, Mama took the silver covers off the dishes and poured tea from the pitcher. I saw how her hands trembled, and I stepped back against the wall so that Christine could not see the tears in my eyes.

"Will you eat, my Christine? There is chicken here. And mashed potatoes."

Christine moaned again.

"I will feed you if you like. Perhaps you will try to drink a little of the hot tea?"

Christine shook her head, but did not open her eyes.

Mama said, "Is a shame to waste good food."

And Mama sat down by the tray and slowly, methodically, she began to eat Christine's lunch.

Christine's eyes flew open. "Mama! What are you doing?"

"Eating your lunch."

"But — but — " Christine sat up in bed. "How can you sit there and eat when I'm — Mama, aren't you worried about me at all?"

Mama shook her head stoically. "You are doing fine. You are just like me. I could never eat, either."

Then Christine began to laugh to herself. She laughed between the spasms of pain, while Mama helped her walk back and forth across the room, and she was still smiling when they wheeled her into the operating room, where she was safely delivered of a seven-pound baby boy.

When Nels came out and said that Christine was fine and that there was nothing more to worry about, Mama's hands stopped trembling.

She leaned on my arm, though, as we walked down the hall to the glass-paned nursery.

A nurse held up a tiny blanketed figure and Mama peered at the wrinkled, yawning little face.

"I think," she said, "he has Papa's nose. And — yes, he has Christine's mouth."

"Oh, Mama! As if you could tell! He looks like a little boiled lobster."

"Why, Katrin — he is a beautiful baby. As you were. All my children were beautiful babies."

166

My thoughts were back in Christine's hospital room.

"Five times," I said wonderingly. "Five times. And all you went through raising us."

"It was good," Mama said.

"How can you say that? Why, I can remember times, Mama — "

"It was good," Mama repeated firmly. "All of it."